"I hate you, Cal de Perregaux!"

Jackie was sobbing with the uncontrollable abandon of a small child. "I honestly hate you!"

"Hey—what's this all about?" whispered Cal in a puzzled voice. "This isn't like you...." His arms enfolded her.

"And why isn't this like me?" she shrieked. "You don't know anything about me! You're too busy throwing your tantrums to care how I might feel! You obviously have no idea what it was like for me...listening to you shouting at those men...and then hearing the vicious things they were doing to you. Not knowing...just imagining..."

"Jackie, I'm sorry. I should have thought—"

"But you didn't," she accused, shoving him away from her. "And why should you? You believe that I'm one of them...that I set you up!"

KATE PROCTOR

sweet captivity

Harlequin Books

TORONTO • NEW YORK • LONDON
AMSTERDAM • PARIS • SYDNEY • HAMBURG
STOCKHOLM • ATHENS • TOKYO • MILAN

Harlequin Presents first edition August 1989
ISBN 0-373-11195-9

Original hardcover edition published in 1988
by Mills & Boon Limited

CHAPTER ONE

'WHAT a silent messenger you are, Miss Jacqueline Templeton; so prim, so very English, despite your excellent command of my language.'

There was amusement on Jackie Templeton's attractive features as she led the tall Frenchman down the badly lit, narrow stairway, but she said nothing.

He certainly had lived up to his reputation of an incorrigible ladies' man, she noted with a wry smile; those grey-green eyes of his had automatically relaxed into lazy flirtation from the moment she had approached him.

'I'd better warn you—if this is one of Claudia's surprise parties, I'm not interested,' he stated suddenly, his tone losing much of its lightness.

At least he had it half right, observed Jackie with silent glee. A surprise was most certainly what he was in for. She turned as they reached the bottom of the stairs and smiled up into the handsome —though now a trifle disgruntled—face. She had no intention of allowing him to back out now she had got him this far.

'I promise you it's not a party, Monsieur de Perregaux . . .'

'Why so formal?' he drawled, those grey-green eyes mocking slightly in their amusement. 'Jacqueline,' he added, softening her name almost to a caress with the deliberately strong French inflection he gave it.

'OK—Pascal,' chuckled Jackie, amused and more than a little surprised to find herself responding quite forcefully to the undoubted physical appeal of the man—an appeal of which he was most certainly aware and which he was exploiting with an almost teasing blatancy.

'My friends call me Cal,' he murmured, giving a small Gallic bow that also happened to bring his dark head closer than necessary to Jackie's gleaming auburn one.

'Come along then, Cal,' she laughed, backing through the swing doors leading into the underground car park. She wondered how many women were fooled by Pascal de Perregaux's mocking parody of the carefree womaniser the French Press had created of one of their leading film directors. Not too many, she hoped, having instantly recognised a shrewdness—an almost cruel detachment—in the inner depths of those flirting eyes.

She was also wondering for just how long he would regard her as a potential friend when he realised what was going on. Then she gave a sigh of relief as she spotted a large red Peugeot moving towards them—at least Henri and the other students were on time. With an apologetic grin, she moved behind the tall Frenchman, giving him a gentle shove in the back as the car doors opened.

'I'm afraid this is the parting of the ways for us, Cal,' she chuckled. 'And try not to be too cross—it's in a very good cause.'

The first thought that crossed her mind as two figures in balaclava helmets leapt out was that they were overdoing things somewhat—masked faces were hardly called for.

Her second thought was that in their enthusiasm to get their quarry into the car, they were man-handling him to an unacceptable degree.

She gave a gasp of protest as she heard the Frenchman's bellow of rage as his head cracked sickeningly against the door rim before he was dragged, struggling and swearing, into the car.

'No! This is . . .' Jackie's angry words of objection turned to a cry of outrage as she was picked up and flung into the dark interior, falling against the furiously struggling man.

'What the hell do you think you're doing?' she shrieked, as the car sped off. Realising that in her agitation she had called out in English, she angrily repeated the words in French. 'Stop this car immediately! Henri—which one of you is Henri?' she yelled, only to be met with complete silence from the three ludicrously masked men. 'You weren't supposed to take me, too! And anyway, you can't . . .' Her words trailed to a horrified gasp as the Frenchman beside her gave a soft moan and fell heavily across her. 'Oh, my God! What have you done to him?' she whispered, fear drying her mouth to sandpaper as one of the men grabbed her roughly by the arm. 'What have . . .' The sharp sting on her arm cut short her words and, for a split second, she was conscious of the now unbearable weight of the man slumped across her . . . pushing her downwards towards a bottomless pit. Then there was nothing.

Someone was holding her arm—in a hold that was neither harsh nor gentle. The fingers that traced patterns up and down her arm were firm and sure—searching, retracing their movements, examining minutely, then moving on.

'What are you doing?' asked Jackie, and wished she had not. Each word had jarred through her head like a marauding army.

'I'm checking for a needle mark.'

He—for the voice was masculine—was checking for a needle mark, relayed a detached part of Jackie to her non-functioning mind. Her mind showed not the slightest interest in this piece of information as it stirred itself to give a fleeting examination of the voice. For a while it dithered with the possibility of the voice having a vague ring of familiarity, then discarded it to examine the excruciating pain pounding in her head.

The pain was so intense that for a moment she felt her body was floating away in its attempt to escape it. Then she discovered points on her body registering outside pressures and that these were the cause of the floating sensation. She was being lifted. Her eyes were tightly shut, as though stapled closed, and it was the fear of sound magnifying the roar of pain in her head that stopped her from crying out in protest as her body was roughly tilted upright.

Then her eyes flew open and protests shrieked from her as caution deserted her with the sudden shock of cold water beating down on her. The water was hurtling into her opened mouth choking her and her cries of outrage.

'Close your mouth—unless you wish to drown.'

The words were spoken in French; soft words that merely made a statement—expressing no interest in her well-being.

Searching for something recognisable through the blear of water, Jackie's eyes fell to the masculine hands harshly grasping her arms and keeping her swaying body upright. As those hands blurred to smears of darkness against the gold of her skin, her gaze rose, struggling to focus through the distortion of cascading water on the masculine face above hers. There was a black satin sleekness to the hair, plastered against the man's head by the relentless flow of water, and a glittering, almost evil watchfulness in the narrowed grey-green eyes trained down on her.

The instant he removed one of those supporting hands, her body sagged, slumping against the solid wet wall of his. As he yanked her viciously upright, the deafening, battering rush of water ceased, leaving in its wake nothing louder than a soft, almost restful gurgle.

'Are you awake now?' enquired that same, chillingly impersonal voice.

Jackie nodded. She was awake, but that was as far as it went—there was little more in her head than that relentless throb of pain.

'Can you walk?'

Again she nodded, wondering where it was they would walk, from where, and who this man was with whom she would make that journey.

The second of her questions was quickly answered as she realised it was a shower out of which they had stepped, but her throbbing head immediately withdrew from the riot of questions that one answer raised.

The second time she stumbled against the tall, broad-shouldered figure whom she blindly followed, he turned and, with an exclamation of impatience, grasped her by the arm and led her into the small room at the end of the corridor. Bringing her to a halt next to one of two beds taking up most of the space in the room, he motioned her to be seated.

'I'll make the covers wet,' she protested, her befuddled mind only now registering the clinging wetness of her clothing. She gave a gasp of bewilderment as he suddenly pushed her down on to the bed.

'Stay there!' barked the man, cold contempt on his handsome, dripping face as he watched her struggle to rise.

His clothing, every bit as wet as her own, clung to his tall, perfectly proportioned body, the dark hairs of his chest visible beneath the clinging transparency of the shirt he unbuttoned, then removed.

Jackie lay her head back against the pillow, the streak of sanity holding her together comforting her with the knowledge that this odd dream would soon pass, while also suggesting that perhaps she should let her hair down and attempt to dry it a little—as was the man now vigorously rubbing the rich, black thickness of his own hair with his discarded shirt.

She had just decided her head would probably explode given a fraction of such treatment when her eyes widened noticeably as her companion calmly unzipped his trousers and stepped out of them. For an instant she was convinced he was also about to remove the white boxer shorts that clung damply to his slim hips, then he merely hitched them up a fraction before seating himself on the edge of the second bed.

'Right—talk,' he ordered softly, the icy disdain on his face contrasting sharply with the unsuppressed fury that burned in his eyes.

Jackie felt herself shiver—not from the clammy wetness of the clothes chilling her body—but a shiver of fear brought on by the look in those piercing eyes and realisation that her mind was a barren wilderness—devoid of all but the swirling clouds of plain misting over her every attempt at thought.

'Who are you? Where are we?' she croaked, wincing with the sharp punishment each word inflicted.

'Don't play games!' he snarled, flinging himself across the gap that separated them and hauling her roughly upright. 'I'm Pascal de Perregaux,' he spat, his fingers biting viciously into the flesh of her arms as he shook her furiously. 'The man you lured into this little set-up with a fictitious message from Claudia Goddard . . .'

'But she knew!' screamed Jackie, pain and awareness exploding in her head. 'Henri said she knew . . . she was helping the students. My head . . . please, my head,' she moaned, slumping against him as the dazzling stark white of the walls surrounding them began spinning to a murky grey.

'Lie down,' he ordered, the anger in his eyes mingling with puzzled suspicion as he caught her sagging body and lowered her back down on the bed.

'Perhaps you should get out of those wet things. There are towels in the bathroom—I'll fetch them.'

Jackie lay back, welcoming the sensation of nothingness slipping over her as she closed her eyes.

'I told you to take these wet things off!' There was no gentleness in the fingers that undid the button at her waistband, nor in the hands that ignored her ineffectual protests and drew the skirt down her legs and off her.

'Stop it . . . I can do it,' she protested weakly as she felt the heavy wetness of her T-shirt being pulled up her body. Shivering and feeling physically sick from the pain still throbbing in her head, Jackie discarded every item of her wet clothing and climbed under the lightweight duvet, clenching her teeth to stop their uncontrolled chattering.

'Your hair—you'd better dry it,' harangued her companion as he returned, and flung a towel at her.

Jackie huddled deeper beneath the covers as she felt the mattress sag with an additional weight.

'Leave me alone,' she moaned, pressing her palms against her temples in an attempt to ease the agony in her head.

'You'll find the headache will ease pretty soon, but I'm sure having your hair scraped back tightly like this can't be helping.'

The hands that unravelled her hair and then began towelling it dry were surprisingly gentle. And though headache was a gross understatement for what she was experiencing—he was right—the acute sharpness of the pain was easing considerably . . . being rapidly replaced by confusion and anxiety.

'What happened?' she exclaimed frantically, struggling to sit up. 'What have they done? I . . .' The words froze on her lips as her eyes met those of the man seated beside her on the bed, hot colour rising to her cheeks as those cold, cruel eyes glanced almost dismissively at her naked breasts before returning to her face.

Hastily raising the quilt to cover herself, Jackie

gave a nervous swallow and continued. 'I think I owe you an explanation . . . of some sort,' she croaked hoarsely, her tongue heavy and swollen and feeling grossly distorted in her mouth.

'That could well be classed as one of the understatements of all time,' he remarked drily, speaking for the first time in faultless, though softly accented, English.

Unnerved by the unremitting vigil of those cold eyes, Jackie too reverted to English. 'I don't know what happened . . . what went wrong . . . why they should behave as they did,' she stammered. 'It's criminal—to drug people . . .'

'You call this an explanation?' he interrupted frigidly.

'It would be easier if you'd stop butting in!' snapped Jackie, and immediately regretted her reaction—he had every reason to be antagonistic. 'You know the fund-raising drive the local students are involved in?'

He frowned, impatiently motioning her to continue.

'I got to know some of the students, and they were most intrigued to learn I was staying at the same hotel as you and your film crew. Some of the stars in your film, including Claudia Goddard, had agreed to help them with publicity once filming was over . . . then Henri, one of the students, told me your film crew had agreed to pay a ransom for you if they could devise a way of kidnapping you . . . as I was staying in the hotel, it was simple for me to give you a fictitious message from Claudia Goddard . . .' Jackie shrugged, conscious of how disjointed her words had sounded as they petered out. Then anger flashed in her eyes as they were caught in the baleful coldness of his stare.

'Would you mind not looking at me as though I were some sort of criminal?' she exploded. 'I can understand how you must be feeling. Do you honestly think I'd have had anything to do with it if I'd known it would turn out like this?'

'Like what?' he sneered. 'Those naughty little students playfully wielding hypodermics? Perhaps they were medical students. So, all this is just harmless fun—part of a fund-raising escapade.' He smiled, a grimace totally devoid of humour. 'What sort of fool do you take me for, Miss Jacqueline Templeton? Did you honestly expect me to believe rubbish like this?'

He rose from the bed, his broad, darkly tanned back to her as he stretched lazily, the muscles of his near-naked body bunching then rippling as his arms rose high above his head. Then he whipped round, catching Jackie off guard with the unexpected speed of his movement as his hands snaked out and dragged her from the bed.

'Enough stories! I want the truth!'

Jackie was oblivious of her nakedness; oblivious of the cruel bite of his fingers on her flesh as he furiously began shaking her again. The only thing of which she was aware was the stabbing shafts of pain returning and now hurtling with renewed intensity through her head.

The low moan of agony torn from her seemed to penetrate his rage. With a vicious oath, he flung her back on to the bed.

'Your pain is in vain,' he told her savagely. 'What am I supposed to believe—that you're not one of them, just because they went to the trouble of doping you, too?'

'Stop it! Stop this, for God's sake!' begged Jackie, her voice rising hysterically as her shaking hands tried to wrap the quilt around her. 'I don't care what you think! I don't care what you believe!' she sobbed. 'But if you touch me again—jar my head just once more—I'll kill you!'

'I doubt if your friends would take kindly to that,' he jeered. 'I'd say I'm obviously worth something to them—alive.'

'Oh, yes, *monsieur,* you are worth a great deal to us—alive.' Jackie's eyes flew open just as Pascal de Perregaux's body whipped round to investigate the origin of those oddly expressionless words.

The speaker was of medium height, stocky and thick-set. What held Jackie riveted was the black cotton balaclava masking his face. How long ago had it been since the sight of such masks on the three men in the car had filled her with nothing more than exasperation? Now she was filled with a stomach-churning fear.

'Who are you, and what the hell do you want?' demanded Pascal de Perregaux, his eyes registering nothing as they fell to the firearm casually held in the man's right hand.

'Who we are and what we want needn't concern you.' Though the man's French was good, his accent was harsh and guttural.

'Surely what you want must concern me,' retorted the scowling Frenchman.

The eyes behind the mask glittered coldly. 'That need only concern those who have the means to provide it—but first they must be given some incentive to provide.' As he spoke, he clicked his fingers and a second, similarly masked man entered, carrying a camera and a newspaper.

'Sit down and display the paper across your chest—the date must be in view,' ordered the stocky man.

Pascal de Perregaux shrugged, his eyes disdainful as he took the paper and sat down.

'What about the woman?' he drawled. 'Isn't she to be included in this little photographic session?'

Neither man showed any signs of having heard those sarcastic words. The first merely looked on as the second took several photographs.

'No—I didn't think she would be,' remarked the Frenchman, a mirthless smile on his lips as his eyes flicked dismissively over Jackie.

The man with the camera, having finished, removed the paper and left.

'You will find everything necessary for your requirements here. Fresh food will be left daily.' The armed man turned to follow the other.

'Wait!' barked Pascal de Perregaux. 'You're forgetting something.'

'I am?'

'Yes—the woman. Take her with you; she's likely to come to harm here.'

It was not so much the threat in those casual words that sent a shiver of fear through Jackie, so much as the strange, almost inhuman glow in the eyes that turned to peer at her through the slits in the mask.

'Your appetite for women is well documented,' murmured that oddly expressionless voice. 'She is here for you to use as you wish—though I should point out that we shall be unable to replace her.'

Jackie's flesh was still crawling long after he had pulled the door to behind him. As her eyes turned to Pascal de Perregaux, they clung in desperation to the tremor of what might have been distaste dying on his handsome features.

'Nice friends you have,' he drawled sarcastically, his words killing any spark of hope in her as he casually swung up his long tanned legs and stretched out on the bed.

'What's wrong with you?' she choked. 'How can you possibly believe I have anything to do with them?'

'Where are we?' he demanded, totally disregarding her words.

'How the hell should I know?' exclaimed Jackie angrily, swathing the quilt around her and getting to her feet.

'Where are you going?'

'I'm going to look around this . . . this cage we're in! And to see what I can do with these,' she added, scooping up her wet clothes. She tried ignoring his presence as he got up and followed her. The fact that he chose to hover an intimidating couple of paces behind her made it next to impossible. 'Are you worried I'll escape?' she exclaimed furiously as she turned in the makeshift kitchen and found her path blocked by his bulk.

'Little chance of that,' he muttered thoughtfully, his eyes scanning the stark, whitewashed walls with their two narrow windows—each painted over in white as were those in the bathroom and bedroom.

She watched as he climbed up on the tumble-dryer that stood next to a washing-machine, and opened one of the tiny windows.

'Same as the others—a high wooden fence, about a metre away from the walls.' He frowned as he leapt down. 'I've a feeling this is an annexe

tacked on to another building . . . with the fence
hiding it.' Suddenly he flashed her a look of pure
loathing. 'I suppose this must be quite entertaining
for you—watching me trying to puzzle out things
that are no doubt completely familiar to you.'
Jackie opened her mouth to plead with him then
gave a shrug of defeat.

'Get your clothes,' she said wearily. 'We might
as well get both lots washed and dried at the same
time.'

'I notice you didn't have to check to see if this
equipment actually works,' he drawled, leaving her
shaking with vexed frustration as he sauntered out.

She had merely assumed the wretched things
would be in working order, she fumed to herself,
hurling her clothes into the washing-machine.

'Here, he muttered, returning and handing her
his wet clothes.

It was on the tip of her tongue to tell him she was
not his servant, when an inner voice of compassion
stopped her. Even though it didn't show, he must
be going through hell . . . what she would be going
through, she realised with a sudden stab of fear,
the moment her mind shook off this odd state of
another-worldliness now possessing it.

'Might as well put these in, too.'

She turned as he spoke, catching the wet garment he tossed at her, and tried hard to stifle her
sharp intake of breath.

The garment she now flung in after the others
was his boxer shorts, and Pascal de Perregaux was
now busily examining the contents of the small
fridge, stark naked.

If he was expecting her to react to his juvenile
attempt to shock, he was going to be disappointed,

she told herself crossly as she filled the soap dispenser and switched on the machine. Nothing happened.

'Seems my guess was wrong,' she informed him smugly. 'It doesn't work.'

'Why not try inserting the plug? That usually helps,' he drawled.

Seething, Jackie did as he suggested.

'Now where do you think you're going?

'For heaven's sake!' shrieked Jackie. 'I'm going to have a shower! Do I need your permission?' Her attempts at dignity as she marched out were seriously hampered by the cumbersome swathe of the quilt around her body.

To her surprise, she found the bathroom well stocked with toiletries, though the presence of a single toothbrush brought it home to her that this small prison had originally been intended for just one prisoner.

And she was wrong to be surprised—her presence here might have been an accident, but whoever had planned the kidnapping of Pascal de Perregaux had done so with meticulous thoroughness.

She could feel the protective cloak of other world-liness slipping from her as she showered and washed her hair. For several minutes she tried to recapture the welcome detachment it had given her. But it was no longer water she felt rushing over her, but fear—a deadly, paralysing fear, chilling through the heat of he water. However unwittingly, she had been party to the kidnapping of one of France's most fêted film directors—a man whose celebrity status would guarantee everything possible would be done to obtain his release. But few would trouble themselves over Jacqueline Templeton, the unknown and foolish English girl but for whom the director might never

have been subjected to this ordeal. They would have
found other ways to get him, protested her terrified
mind—had they needed to.

Having towelled her hair almost dry and combed it
out, Jackie wrapped herself in a towel, her hands
fumbling they shook so badly.

The cold eyes of the man lying on one of the beds,
a towel draped across his hips, flickered over the slim
figure entering the room.

'You don't have to knock,' he informed her, his
eyes lingering on the rich auburn cloud that hung
past her shoulders, softly framing a face that hovered
on the brink of beauty yet fell short—not from any
structural defect, but from a lack of something
almost indefinable—as though some vital spark had
been stripped from it.

Jackie went to the bed she now regarded as hers,
her slim, tanned shoulders hunching slightly as she
sat down. 'Please . . . couldn't we at least try to talk?'
she began.

'There's coffee made if you want some,' he
muttered, draining the mug he held, then holding it
out to her. 'You can refill mine while you're at
it—black, no sugar.'

'Look—I know how you must be feeling—I'd be
suspicious too if I were you,' blurted out Jackie as
she took the mug.

'Why don't you just get the coffee? Then . . .' He
paused.

'Then we can talk?' she pleaded, hope glimmering
in her eyes.

He shrugged. 'Why talk?' he drawled, suddenly
switching to French. 'I thought we could make
love—there's precious little else for us to do.'

Without uttering a single word, Jackie rose and

walked out of the room.

The tears that scalded their way down her cheeks had little to do with the insult intended by his mocking suggestion—it was just the way he had chosen to express himself that had triggered a long-forgotten memory—a memory that now stirred up the terrible, aching despair that not one minute of the past few weeks had been able to diminish.

Suddenly she was seeing Nadine's warm brown eyes, twinkling despite the dark smudges of pain beneath them even then—how many years ago had it been?

'One day you will need to remember that when a Frenchman says he wants to kiss you, *ma petite,* he is suggesting you make love.' There had been a ruefully indulgent chuckle in her soft voice. 'Only my incorrigible countrymen would have the gall to corrupt the innocent verb "to kiss" into a blatant sexual overture.'

'Nadine, if you could only know how I miss you,' whispered Jackie, scrubbing the tears from her cheeks with the back of her hand before pouring the coffee.

Time was acclaimed as the universal healer, she reminded herself, and found no comfort in the reminder. For twelve years—for half her life—that beautiful, bountiful, perfect Frenchwoman had been so much more than an aunt by marriage. Nadine had been mother, sister, friend to her. Nadine had been the mainspring of her life, and her death still overshadowed everything, rendering even the horrifying predicament in which she now found herself almost trivial by comparsion.

CHAPTER TWO

SOON he would finish the press-ups, then he would start swinging from the door-frame like an ape.

There was nothing remotely ape-like about the glistening, perfectly proportioned body exercising on the floor between the two beds, though there was nothing remotely resembling appreciation in Jackie's eyes as they flickered over him.

Both her teeth and her hands clenched involuntarily as he rose and went over to the doorway—just as she had predicted. With a bit of luck the door-frame would collapse under the weight of him, she thought testily, restlessly shifting her long, shapely legs on top of the bed. Just watching him was exhausting, she told herself listlessly, and only a complete nutcase would dream of exercising in heat like this.

She lifted the hem of the perspiration-dampened black T-shirt clinging to her body, and flapped it in a vain attempt to create a cooling breeze. Apart from a pair of white briefs, it was the only garment she wore.

Much more of this and she would be a gibbering wreck!

For two days now they had been incarcerated. Each morning a masked and terrifyingly armed man had silently deposited foodstuffs in the make-shift kitchen. And, without even bothering to consult Pascal de Perregaux, she had taken over the cooking—it was one of the few things she had to relieve the terrible monotony. A monotony made worse by the fact that they now barely spoke to one another, since her every attempt at reasoning with him had been countered by his blatant sexual propositioning of her. But now her nerve was threatening to snap as, she felt certain, his soon would too. She could sense the tension building up in him, and deep down knew this almost manic exercising he indulged in was an out-let for the volatile energy within him.

And God help her when he finally blew, she warned herself with positive stirrings of fear; to him she was the enemy.

Perspiration was gleaming on his body as he dropped lightly to his feet and flexed his shoulders.

'Cal,' she called to him, determined to have her say before he disappeared for one of his innumer-able showers, and before her nerve deserted her.

'Jacqueline.'

'Has it never occurred to you that you could be wrong—that I'm telling the truth?' she blurted out, wanting to kick herself for the accusation in her tone when she had wanted to sound reasonable.

'It occurs to me now and then, but I have little trouble dismissing it.' He turned and walked out of the room, and a few seconds later she heard the sound of the shower.

She lay back, her eyes closing against the stark monotony of the ceiling—white, like the walls; like every door in her prison; white, like the blankness beneath her lids as hopelessness engulfed her completely.

'Perhaps it *would* be an idea if we talked.'

Jackie's eyes flew open, she was startled to hear

his voice beside her. His hair and body now glistened from the shower. But what widened her eyes in puzzlement was the mug of coffee he held out to her—the first gesture he had ever made towards her that had been remotely sociable.

'The way I feel at the moment, it would take very little to push me over the edge,' he told her quietly, his eyes, as ever, guarded and watchful.

'I know,' muttered Jackie, trying not to grimace as she took a sip of the coffee she found far too strong and which contained no milk.

'Just a small thing could do it,' he added almost as though he were addressing himself. 'Such as that steak you cooked. I eat my steaks charred on the outside—raw in the middle. And as for salads . . .' He blinked as though surprised, hastily stepping aside as Jackie hurled the mug to the floor at his feet, smashing it to tiny pieces and sending out a spray of hot liquid that gleamed against the dark hairs of his legs before trickling down to join the spreading puddle on the floor.

'Do you think I give a damn about how you like your meat?' she screamed in English. 'Or how you want your bloody salads prepared? I'm a human being—yes, a human being—and I'm desperately frightened! I'm trying to hang on to my sanity in the middle of a terrible nightmare. And you're the person who's going to detroy me—not those ghastly men with their guns and masks—but you, the one person in whom I should be able to find at least a shred of comfort . . .'

'Jacqueline . . .'

'Nobody calls me Jacqueline! Only you—the man who subjects me to his own brand of cynical sexual harassment every time I open my mouth to explain. The terrible thing is there's nothing I *can* explain . . .'

'Jackie, there's no need to shout. I'm not deaf.'

'Oh, but you are, Pascal de Perregaux,' she retorted, her voice dropping to a hoarse whisper. 'You're deaf and blind and devoid of anything remotely approaching human decency!' As the words tumbled from her, she clutched her arms tightly around her in an attempt to still the violent trembling now racking her body.

'I doubt if there's any comfort I could offer you—even had I wanted to,' he stated emotionlessly. 'If it's money they want, my family probably has the means—assuming the demands are within the bounds of reason.' He shrugged, kicking aside the debris surrounding him with a bare foot as he sat on the edge of his bed.

'Whereas I have no family—no money,' said Jackie tonelessly.

While her own eyes flickered over the mess on the floor, she could feel his on her in the silence that followed. Which of the two looks would be in his eyes, she wondered half-heartedly as she felt the spirit draining from her, the pure loathing, or the cold mockery that accompanied his drawled propositioning? Pride rekindled her spirit as she remembered the deliberately insulting sweep of those cold eyes over her body.

'Just to save you the trouble of suggesting it yet again—no, I'm not interested in a bout of sexual athletics to while away the time,' she stated through clenched teeth.

'Sorry to disappoint you,' he murmured, the merest suspicion of humour in his tone. 'But I was about to ask what you do—what sort of job you have.'

'I haven't a job.'

'You haven't a job now—or you just don't work?'

'I haven't worked,' she stated, wondering why on earth a tinge of defiance had crept into her voice . . . there was a very good reason why she had never worked.

'You have no job—no money—yet you were staying in one of the most exclusive hotels in France, let alone Biarritz.'

'Yes!' she flashed. 'But you know me— I'm a criminal!'

'You're prepared to admit it now?'

'Of course I'm not!' She gave a groaned travesty of a laugh as she flung herself back down on the bed. 'But what's the point in my telling you I was staying there . . . on a sort of private pilgrimage?' she asked despondently.

She looked over as she heard his bed creak. He was lying at full stretch, his hands clasped behind his head. And for one vivid moment she was remembering the light-hearted flirtation that had been in his eyes and his voice that fateful day she had approached him. *'My friends call me Cal.'* Had she even admitted to herself then how strong her initial attraction towards him had been? It had been disconcertingly strong, but then, few men had ever crossed her path with the looks and dynamism of Pascal de Perregaux.

'Jackie, if you don't tell me, how can you possibly expect me to reassess my judgement?' he asked, his tone for once reasonable. 'You can take your time, that's one thing you and I have plenty of,' he sighed. 'So, tell me of your pilgrimage,

Jackie . . . but first, tell me how it is you speak almost faultless French.'

She hesitated. He could hardly realise it, but he had just about asked her to tell him her life-story. But he had called her Jackie, and because she so desperately needed something—anything—she could cling to, she took it as an olive branch.

'My aunt—Nadine—is . . . was French.'

'Was? When did she die?'

The baldness of his words sent a shiver of recoil through her.

'Three months . . . no, eleven weeks ago.'

'You and she were close?'

Close? What sort of word was that to describe the relationship that had been hers and Nadine's?

'No. We were so much more than close,' she whispered, closing her eyes and letting the memories flood in. 'Nadine was married to my Uncle James—my father's elder brother. Nadine and James and my parents were very close . . . we often took holidays together. When I was twelve, we had our summer holiday in Italy.' She should never have started telling him this, she thought as she felt an almost suffocating tightness creep into her chest. 'That year, a group of terrorists mined one of the mainline railway tracks . . . we were on the train that detonated it. My mother and father and my uncle were killed. Nadine and I survived.' How much words could hide. But they could never disguise what remained within her, barely diminished by the passing of time . . . those terrifying, slow-motion hours when Nadine's tortured body had shielded and protected hers until rescue had come.

'You survived—but the mental scars must have

been appalling,' he stated quietly.

'For years . . . I couldn't bear Nadine to be out of my sight. Even when I was eighteen, she had to resort to emotional blackmail to make me go to university . . . saying I had to prove her worth as my French teacher by getting a good degree.'

'Was it your fear of being separated from her that stopped you getting a job?'

'No—by the time I'd finished my degree I was over that. But by then Nadine's health had deteriorated badly.The injuries she had sustained in Italy were severe—they were what eventually killed her. She was confined to a wheelchair within a couple of years of the disaster . . . though mercifully she suffered little in the way of physical pain.'

'And your pilgrimage to Biarritz? Is that where your aunt came from?'

'No—it was there she first met James. They were both in their thirties, each too busy enjoying life to the full to have ever contemplated anything as mundane as marriage. They were married here—in Biarritz, I mean—within ten days of meeting . . . they were like a couple from a fairy-tale . . . so beautiful and so happy together. And so much of her died with James . . . yet she held on for my sake. I suppose in a way I was all she had left of him.'

'But what made you come to Biarritz?'

'A few weeks before she died, she began speaking a lot about the place . . . of the joy she had found there.'

'But it was James who brought her the joy—not the place.'

'I know that . . . but when she was gone . . .'

She hesitated. 'I can't explain it . . . I had to come.'

'And look what you found,' he stated grimly. 'But one thing's for sure, we're no longer in Biarritz—it's far too hot. I'd say we're a lot further south.'

'You've no idea how long it took—getting here?' she asked, a stillness in her that waited in trepidation for him to revert to cold tormentor now that the subject touched on their plight.

'I came to on this bed about seven hours after they'd knocked me out. I've no idea how long I'd been here. It took you another couple of hours to come round.'

'But you weren't entirely convinced they'd drugged me, too,' she stated tentatively.

'No—not until I saw you were experiencing the same vicious headache I'd woken up to.' He turned to face her, his eyes inscrutable. 'And even then, you could have been instructed in what symptoms to display.' The edge of his voice frightened her with its threat to demolish the truce between them she so desperately needed.

'I do understand how you feel,' she whispered, pleading. 'Cal, I know I have no right to ask—considering this terrible thing I've done to you—but could you perhaps try to give me the benefit of your doubts?'

'God knows, I'm trying!' he exclaimed, rising to a sitting position. 'But you don't make it easy! I'm sure few would describe you as a fool—yet only someone of monumental stupidity would agree to the stunt you claim to have taken part in. It was terrorists who wrecked your family all those years ago! Kidnapping is no longer a prank students can indulge in—not in the political climate in which we now live—and certainly not when the intended victim is a de Perregaux.'

'You're right . . . I can only agree with every word you say,' she admitted wretchedly. 'But I don't understand the significance of your family name. I take it there's more to it than your fame as a film director.'

He gave a humourless laugh. 'A little,' he murmured drily. 'There was a time they'd have been happier had I worked under a pseudonym—the French aristocracy have some pretty intransigent views on what it and isn't acceptable for their members.'

'But your work is highly respected—revered, even,' protested Jackie.

'It wasn't so much my directing films they objected to,' he chuckled, a low, infectious chuckle that was like music to her ears. 'It was what occurred in my second film that gave them the vapours.'

'I've only seen two of your films—Nadine couldn't visit cinemas, so we got what we could on video.'

He shook his head when she named the two she had seen. 'No, it was *Applause* that had half the family wanting me disinherited. Not my immediate family, though—they were rather amused.' He leaned back against the head-rest, a reminiscent grin softening the harsh beauty of his features.

'Aren't you going to tell me what it was—this terrible thing that gave half your family the vapours?' coaxed Jackie. He was more relaxed now than she had ever seen him, and it was a moment she would give anything to prolong.

'You'd no doubt understand if ever you saw it,'

he murmured, and for an instant she caught a gleam of what might have been teasing in the eyes that flickered towards her then away.

'That's not fair,' she protested, a slight breathlessness in her voice as her heart unaccountably skipped several beats.

He shrugged, then gave another of those soft chuckles. 'I'm a perfectionist when it comes to my work. There was a scene in the film—a little cameo of a role—that called for a gigolo stripping from full evening-dress down to nothing. It was a great scene, one of the best jazz saxophonists of all time had written a blues piece to accompany it. Hell, I must have auditioned over fifty actors for the role—and not one of them could give what was required.' The long, silky, black lashes fluttered upwards, the eyes beneath them twinkling with mischief as they met hers. 'In the end I did the scene myself—brilliantly!'

Jackie gave a chuckle of delighted disbelief. 'And the de Perregaux family objected to one of their own displaying his all?'

'You do my illustrious family a disservice if that's what you think,' he chided, with a wickedly appealing grin. 'No—what they found so grossly offensive was that one of theirs was portraying a gigolo!'

'Did they ever manage to forgive you?' she asked, trying to close her mind to the welter of vivid and disturbingly erotic pictures now filling it. Perhaps he did have an undeniably magnificent body—God knew, she had seen enough of it—but what was equally undeniable was that their unnatural enforced intimacy was beginning to have a most disconcerting effect on her.

'Oh, they forgave me—they're a fairly compassionate lot and they saw the terrible price I was paying for my folly.'

Jackie's eyes flickered questioningly to his. There was that laughter in his voice again —intimate and almost sexy in its husky softness—and something told her this man, apart from all his other attributes, possessed a sense of humour few would find easy to resist.

'For a while I seemed to become the eighth wonder of the world—women would lurk in their hordes, literally leaping on me out of the blue . . . I'd no idea they could be so aggressive. And the fan mail I received—my God, most of it was downright pornographic!'

Jackie found herself weak with laughter at the sight of the exaggerated outrage on his face. She raised her fingers to her cheek, almost as though to wipe away tears from her laughter, and that small gesture brought her inexplicably back to reality. They were out of their minds! They were laughing, actually laughing, while all the time the threat of the unknown hung over them . . . a threat that terrorised like a death sentence.

'Jackie?' His face had tensed, the laughter slipping from it as though it had never been.

'Cal . . . how can we possibly laugh? We don't know why we're here, or what could eventually happen to us. How can you be so calm? It's not natural!'

'You think I'm calm?' he asked woodenly. 'All I'm doing is trying to hold a paralysing, gut-aching fear at bay . . . I, who have never known the true meaning of fear.' He sat up, swinging his feet to the floor. 'Their not saying what it is they want is a form of extreme mental torture . . . it disorientates the mind, making thinking even an hour ahead an impossibility. I've no idea how long the human mind can cope with the pressure of such total uncertainty.' He rose, carefully avoiding the jagged pieces of china on the floor as he moved away from the beds. 'And for that reason, laughter is all I . . . you and I . . . have to help us sublimate.' There was a haggard pallor beneath the gold of his tan as he gazed bleakly across at her. 'Jackie, for as long as we can, you and I will have to hang on to what laughter we can create, it may be our only salvation.'

That he had offered her a truce against his instincts was at times nerve-rackingly apparent. It was a truce of fragility and unpredictability, faltering in those tense moments when the watchful coldness would creep back into his eyes, and when Jackie could only watch helplessly till the conflict raging in him subsided.

But those moments grew fewer as the heat in their small prison swelled to an enervating oppressiveness.

'We've got to do something about getting those windows opened,' he exclaimed wearily as they sat on the stone floor of the corridor—the coolest place they could find.

Jackie shrugged. They had spent hours trying to override the fiendish spring-loaded mechanism that prevented the tiny windows opening more than a few useless centimetres.

'We could try wedging them with the cutlery again—except that we're now down to a couple of forks, one spoon and one knife,' she muttered, listlessly lifting the hem of her T-shirt and fanning her stomach, oblivious of the eyes that widened momentarily at the sight of the tanned flatness of her stomach, the stark whiteness of her skimpy briefs accentuating the rich gold of her skin.

'It doesn't work,' exclaimed Cal impatiently, rising to his feet. 'I suggest we smash the bloody things—at least that way we'll get some air.'

Jackie looked up at the tall, scowling figure. He was serious. 'We'll use the frying pan,' she grinned, accepting the hand he stretched out to her. 'It'll be a pleasure—smashing part of this place to smithereens!'

'The trouble is,' he chuckled, keeping imprisoned the hand by which he had helped her up, 'there are five windows.'

'Two each,' retorted Jackie, having problems with her speech as her facial muscles treacherously froze on her. 'And the fifth goes to the one making the best job of his or her two.'

They were so close, she felt certain he must feel the rustle of her breath against the dark hairs of his chest. And so close, the smell of him—the special way his body seemed to take the scent of the soap they both used and imbue it with a spicy masculinity of his own—was filling her nostrils like a heady incense.

'And who's going to decide which of us has made the best job?' he asked softly.

'I'm sure the results will speak for themselves,' she laughed unsteadily, tearing free her hand and racing to the kitchen. Her heart was pounding with a heavy, uncomfortable thud as she got out the frying pan. It was this completely unnatural enforced intimacy that was affecting her, she told herself. She was living cheek by jowl with an exceptionally attractive man—eating together, sharing the same bedroom, spending every minute of every hour of every day together.

'I'll take first crack—or should I say smash?' he grinned, taking the pan from her and leaping agilely on to the washing-machine top.

His legs were so long and slim and beautifully proportioned, she thought dreamily as he straightened up. Hell, she told herself disgustedly, she could hardly keep her eyes off him—if she carried on like this much longer, it would soon be her hands! Her disturbing observations were brought to a shrieked halt as he took aim and smashed the tiny window, sending white-painted glass showering everywhere.

'Cal, for heaven's sake, not like that!' she protested, laughing. 'The glass is supposed to end up outside, not in here. I forgot to tell you, we're each clearing up our own mess!'

'Nadine, what sort of a Frenchwoman were you?' he groaned. 'You brought this girl up with the wrong attitude!'

'If the wrong attitude is being prepared to clear up your mess after you, you're right,' murmured Jackie, oddly disconcerted by his unexpected mention of Nadine.

'You shouldn't mind me mentioning her, she was a central part of your life,' he stated softly, sitting himself on top of the machine and letting his long legs swing. 'You should talk about her more. You can't lock her away as though she had never existed, just because remembering brings pain.'

'No,' she sighed, taking the pan from him. 'That's something she believed strongly, too. From the start of our life together, we always spoke of

my parents and James . . . till in the end there was
more happiness than pain in the remembering . . .
that's one of the many things that was so special
about her . . .'

'None the less, I'm sure she'd be appalled by
your treatment of one of her countrymen,' he
retorted, deliberately lightening the conversation.
'It's humiliating enough your having had me
slaving over this washing-machine—but now,
sweeping floors!'

Jackie could almost hear Nadine's earthly
chuckle floating around them. Of one thing there
could be no doubt, Nadine would have been
thoroughly delighted by this wickedly attractive
countryman of hers.

'I'll do a deal with you, Cal,' she chuckled,
clambering up on to the sink. 'If I make a fraction
of the mess you've just made, I'll do the clearing
up.'

'It's a deal,' he grinned complacently. 'Mean-
while, I'll stay here—till you've cleared up. I've
delicate feet.'

Tossing him a pitying smile, Jackie began
tapping gently with the pan till eventually she was
able to push all the glass to the outside.

'Get the broom, de Perregaux, and start sweeping,' she laughed.

'But at least I enjoyed myself,' he retorted,
climbing down. 'Come on, Jackie, let yourself
go! Let's really smash the bedroom windows to
bits!'

It took no more than those laughing words to
persuade her, though her enjoyment had begun to
pall a little when, half an hour after clearing up the
considerable mess they had created, she still found

her feet picking up agonising little slivers of glass.

'You and your bright ideas,' she complained, hobbling to the shower and turning it on full blast. She sat down cross-legged beneath its cooling cascade, morosely examining the soles of her feet.

'Stop being such a baby and move over,' he ordered, almost unbalancing her as he heaved himself in beside her. 'Come on, give me a foot and I'll make it all better.'

He grinned through the water that gushed over him, plastering his hair like a black satin cap to his head as he grabbed one of her feet and began soaping it vigorously.

'Ouch! That's agony!' she shrieked, struggling to withdraw her foot.

'I thought I told you to stop being such a baby.' He yanked her foot up, bringing it closer to his face, and proceeded to remove two pieces of glass.

'How can you see what you're doing?' demanded Jackie, now suffocatingly aware of their casual entanglement—of the powerful masculinity of the sleek, wet body huddled by hers, and suddenly of the clearly defined outline of her own body against the clinging wetness of her T-shirt.

'I can see clearly . . . so very clearly,' he whispered, drawing her towards him till her body straddled his. 'I can see those firm, round breasts of yours, covered by their thin film of black.'

There was a hot darkness in his eyes as his hands slowly drew up her clinging T-shirt, and there was a soft moan in his throat as she lifted her arms unhesitatingly to accommodate him, allowing him to remove the redundant garment completely.

For an instant, he twisted away from her, stemming the flow that gushed over them. Then his hands and those hot, yearning eyes returned to her.

'Is it the cold of the water that gives these ruby-red nuggets their hardness?' he asked huskily, his fingers tracing the outer circle of each breast.

Jackie was unsure when her arms had reached out to link round his neck. But her eyes were locked against the darkness of the fingers moving against the paleness of her breasts—fingers that traced tantalising patterns with the shivering lightness of their touch, moving in ever decreasing circles. Her breath was trapped inside her, waiting as her body waited, then bursting from her in a sharp cry of pleasure and shock as those fingers moved to where her body had beckoned, capturing and teasing against her nipples, bringing them to rigid peaks of desire that swelled and strained beneath the almost unbearable delight of his touch.

Then his hands were covering her breasts, their palms kneading and impatient as her body arched, her arms tightening compulsively round his neck.

'Cal!' she moaned, a choked cry of pleading.

'Kiss me, Jackie,' he demanded, his hand sliding round her back, pressing her to him as the wet, silky softness of his chest hairs moved sensuously against her aching breasts.

Her hands reached up to cradle his head, drawing his face down to hers.

'Silence all my doubts with the sweetness of your kisses,' he breathed raggedly, his mouth brushing impatiently against hers, parting her lips to receive the hot, probing hunger of his. She had been kissed before, but never like this. Never as though she were being invaded and possessed; never with such reckless, igniting passion that now drove her tongue to explore as his did, searching and seeking, familiarising and rejoicing.

His every touch sent sensations of almost unbearable pleasure rocketing through her, filling her with an insatiable need as her legs locked around his back and her hands began a frantic exploration of his face, his neck, the exciting play of muscle that rippled across his shoulders—each touch never enough, each leading to a need for more.

Then his fingers were sinking into her hair, drawing back her head, arching her body for him to bury his face at her breasts. And she was lost, drowning in the sensation of longing and excitement with which she was being bombarded, his mouth and tongue goading her to a fever of madness while the exquisite punishment of his teeth against her flesh brought wild, incoherent cries shuddering to her lips.

'Hold on to me,' he whispered huskily, his arms tightening around her as he drew himself to his feet. Then his mouth was reclaiming hers, bruising with the savage urgency of its possession as her legs slowly uncurled from around him, sliding against the wetness of him till she, too, was on her feet. And, even as he was drawing her against him, her body was seeking his, discovering and wantonly abandoning itself to the rigid heat of desire that seemed to burn through her flesh.

'Cal,' she whispered, her hands, with a will of their own, sliding past the damp elastic at his waistband to revel in the firm, cool flesh beneath them that moved with the slow, sensuous sway of his hips. 'I don't care about anything . . . nothing except this moment.'

'Something told me I'd find the fire of passion in you,' he whispered hoarsely. 'That you would want me with the same strength I've wanted you.' There was a slight tremor in the hand that reached up to stroke aside stray strands of hair from her face. 'Jackie, I take it you're adequately protected,' he murmured, his lips nuzzling against the corner of her mouth.

'Adequately what?' she whispered, too distracted by the shivering excitement of his breath against her face for words to have any meaning.

He gave a soft groan, then drew her acquiescent body from the fierce heat of his.

'No!' she protested, her arms clinging.

'Jackie—the pill, the coil, anything! If you have no form of contraceptive protection . . . I'll drown myself!' he groaned.

Jackie flung herself at him, clinging in desperation as she violently shook her head. 'There must be something you can do! There must be!' she pleaded.

'Hell, we're a great pair,' he groaned, hugging her fiercely to him. 'I'm afraid there's nothing I can do—except this.'

Jackie gave a cry of disbelief and shock as the water began cascading down on them once more.

'We might as well both drown,' he added with a morose laugh.

CHAPTER THREE

'YOU'RE perfectly capable of cooking meat the way I like it; why have you ruined it again?' complained Cal, depositing his plate on the floor with an expression of disgust.

Jackie hunched her shoulders in angry defiance.

'Cook it yourself if you don't like the way I do it,' she retorted acidly, refusing to admit, even to herself, that the meat had all the appeal of charred leather.

They were both seated on the kitchen floor—a table and chairs having obviously been deemed unnecessary items by their captors—each clad in a towel as their clothes churned noisily in the washing-machine.

'And did you have to put that bloody machine on? It only creates more heat!' he snapped.

'What did your last slave die of?' snarled Jackie, leaping up and dumping her full plate in the sink. 'I've had enough of this!' She flounced her way to the bedroom, flinging herself disconsolately on her bed.

Whinge, whinge, whinge—that was all he had done since . . . With a groan of frustration, she grabbed the pillow and slammed it over her head.

'Go away!' she yelled, as she felt the pillow being tugged from her. 'Just go away—and pick on someone your own size.'

'I wish I could, but you know that's not possible,'

41

chided a chuckling voice as the bed creaked beneath his weight. 'Jackie, I've put on some coffee . . .'

'I hate your coffee!'

'I've made it weak and putrid, just as you like it.'

'I don't like it weak,' she retorted. 'It's just that you drink it like treacle.' She hurled herself upright, then immediately wished she hadn't as the mere sight of him started up that terrible aching longing in her. 'Oh, Cal, what's happening to us?' she wailed, the words spilling out of her unchecked.

'What's happening to us is a painful dose of sexual frustration,' he sighed.

'Speak for yourself!' she retorted, forced to because even now her mind perversely refused to acknowledge the fact that a few hours ago she had blatantly begged this man to make love to her, no matter what.

'Oh, no. I'm speaking for both of us,' he whispered, his arms taking her. 'Aren't I, Jackie?'

His chin was making small circular movements on the top of her head as she froze to a ramrod tenseness in his arms.

'I hate you!' she hissed, not daring to allow a single muscle to move. 'I hate you,' she murmured huskily, her head tilting back to see his face as her arms slid round his naked torso.

She saw the compulsive tightening of his jaw as he tried to fight the hot darkness that flared in his eyes.

'Why do you make me feel like a gauche adolescent?' he demanded hoarsely. 'Why do I have to reassure myself that you want me—when it's only torturing me—when your frustrated bitchiness tells me beyond doubt?'

'If I was being bitchy—what's the word for what you were being?' she choked, the air squeezed from her lungs by the sweet agony of the sensations filling her.

'Jackie, this is getting us nowhere,' he sighed, regret diluting the desire in his gaze as he slipped free from the beckoning of her arms and stood up. 'I'll see if the coffee's ready.'

'Don't bother to come back!' she yelled after him, flinging herself down once more.

The way she was behaving was appalling her—yet she seemed to have no power to control it. It was almost as though she had stepped out of her body—a body that had become a stranger to her with the explosive violence of its new awakening—and now she watched like a helpless spectator.

She had to pull herself together, she warned, making a concentrated effort to do just that. The conditions they were being subjected to were enough to affect the sanest of minds . . . she had to salvage something of her rapidly diminishing pride. She leapt up and ran to the kitchen.

'Cal, I'm sorry!' she burst out, protests immediately raging in her mind as the familiar melting need began sweeping through her. 'I don't know why I'm behaving like this—it's just not me!'

'Do you think I don't realise that?' he asked gently, passing her a mug and grimacing as he took a sip from his own.

'Let me make you some more—stronger,' she offered, softer and infinitely more disturbing feelings welling up in her.

'This is fine,' he lied, strolling into the corridor

and sprawling on to the floor. 'At least we've managed to create a suspicion of a draught,' he murmured drily, as she joined him.

They drank in silence, Jackie pessimistically deciding that all it would take would be one wrong word from him—then she would snap competely.

'Jackie, you have to understand it's illogical to feel embarrassed by the strength of your physical need. Our circumstances are heightening all our senses to an extreme.' There was gentleness in his eyes as he turned and looked down at her troubled face. 'Neither of us has acknowledged it, but each morning every nerve in our bodies is tuned almost to snapping point by the awaiting of something as mundane as the delivery of the food . . . for us, nothing is mundane. The day before yesterday they arrived at midday for their second photographic session . . . yesterday and today, as noon approached, do you think I wasn't conscious of the tension building up in you, Jackie, a tension mirrored by my own?'

'But how much longer can we take it?' she asked hopelessly.

He shrugged. 'It's too bad that the only pleasure to be had from all this heightened awareness is one that's to be denied us,' he murmured wryly.

Jackie remained silent. His words were pretty much those she had needed to hear—yet they had left her feeling oddly dissatisfied.

'At least you were responsible enough to be aware of that,' she muttered guiltily, horrified by her own complete lack of responsibility.

'We men are pretty selfish creatures, always expecting women to take the precautions—in serious relationships, anyway. My brother's poor wife was as sick as a dog when she tried taking the pill.'

'She has my sympathies,' exclaimed Jackie. 'I felt like death for the few months I was on it—but at least it did the trick.'

As the implications of what she had just said dawned on her, it was on the tip of her tongue to explain. She opened her mouth, then closed it. There seemed something slightly ludicrous about discussing her early teenage menstrual problems with the sophisticated man of the world seated beside her.

'Jackie . . . what's your attitude to abortion?'

For a moment she wondered if she had heard correctly. 'I'm not sure—except that I certainly don't see it as a form of contraception,' she stated woodenly. She was scarcely what could be described as an experienced woman, but she had difficulty imagining herself having this conversation with any of the men she knew. But Pascal de Perregaux was a man apart from any she had ever met.

'Jackie, no matter what any man might say about being careful—it doesn't work . . . even if he has the self-control to attempt it.'

'Cal—could I ask you something? It isn't meant as a criticism.'

'Ask away.'

'You seem unusually preoccupied with contraception—I'd even say inordinately so, for a man.'

'I can't say it's something I've ever discussed with other men,' he stated, giving her a peculiarly blank look for one with such expressive eyes. 'Because the woman is the one who physically bears the child doesn't alter the fact that the child is fifty per cent the flesh and blood of its father.'

'And fifty per cent de Perregaux blood would, no doubt, set it way above the common herd,' she murmured drily.

'No doubt,' he drawled, a coldness in his eyes as he rose and glanced down at her. 'Do you want more coffee—before I make some that's drinkable?'

'I'll make it,' she offered, leaping up and taking his mug. 'Cal, I'm sorry, I . . .'

'Why be sorry, Jackie, when you hit the nail right on the head?'

'Stop it! You're so sarcastic . . . so damned . . .'

'Frustrated!' He clutched his heart, his eyes rolling theatrically. 'Only a Frenchman could die of frustration,' he declared, speaking English with a grossly exaggerated French accent.

'And only a Frenchman could massacre the English language like that,' quipped Jackie, overwhelmingly relieved by his quicksilver change of mood.

'My accent may not be as good as yours,' he murmured, catching hold of her by the hair and dragging her into the kitchen after him. 'But my English grammar is perfect—whereas your French grammar . . .'

'What's wrong with my grammar?' she demanded indignantly, tugging free and pouring herself more coffee. 'Cal, where did you learn to speak such good English?'

'Don't change the subject,' he taunted, then grinned angelically. 'Unlike the British aristocracy, we French are not averse to alien cultures . . .'

'Liar! Both nationalities have that ghastly habit of talking loudly in their respective languages—expecting foreigners to understand.

And it doesn't just apply to the aristocracy, either!'

'Do you wish to hear where I learned my immaculate English or not?'

'Yes.'

'Yes, you do, or yes, you don't?'

'Cal!'

'At Cambridge—I read French Literature there.'

'That's cheating!'

'No, it isn't. Doing it through English was pretty tortuous . . . but you have to admit, my English is perfect.'

'Is there anything about yourself you consider anything less than perfect?' asked Jackie sweetly, and gave a groan of exasperation as an expression of deep concentration immediately settled on his face.

She watched as he began preparing the coffee, that expression remaining on his face as he did his best to mask his laughing eyes. And, as she watched, she felt that new, softer feeling wash over her—the same feeling that had come to her when he had begun drinking the coffee he obviously couldn't abide.

'Cal . . . I don't even know if you're married.' The words slipped out, startling her.

'I'm not. What makes you ask?'

She turned away from the scrutiny of those amused eyes as she felt hot colour rush to her cheeks.

'I was just thinking—with a little more practice, you'll make some lucky person quite a passable wife.'

'A passable what?' he growled through laughter, his hands heavy on her shoulders as he spun her to face him. 'Jackie, I . . . oh, God!' he groaned softly, crushing her fiercely against him. 'This is inhuman!' He buried his face against hers, his breath a hot shiver against her skin.

'Cal, don't . . . please,' she begged, clenching her hands by her side as she fought the compulsion to fling her arms around him and drown in the excitement of him. 'Cal, I . . .'

They both froze as they heard the familiar sounds that heralded the opening of the solid metal door built into the wall. Cal straightened then moved her so that she stood behind him as the door swung slowly open.

This time three men stepped into the room, all three wearing the inevitable masks, two armed. It was the familiar, stocky figure in the middle who was unarmed—in his hands he carried a cordless telephone and a single sheet of paper.

'Read this,' he ordered handing Cal the paper then placing the telephone on the work surface.

The Frenchman's eyes flickered over the sheet before settling coldly on the man.

'I said, read it.'

'I have—or are you asking me to read it aloud?' drawled Cal.

His answer was a vicious blow across the side of his face, and Jackie heard her own strangled cry as she watched blood trickle down his cheek. She saw the heavily ornate ring on the hand that had struck the blow just as she felt her wrist taken in Cal's warning grasp.

'Now—read it.'

For God's sake, do as he asks, begged Jackie silently as she saw those broad shoulders tense to give their familiar dismissive shrug.

'OK.' He completed the shrug. 'Do—everything—they—ask,' he read, much as an

irritating child might read out in class.
'You—will—never—see—me—alive—if—you—
don't . . . God, this is straight out of a comic,' he
added in an aside in English, and received another
vicious blow across the face for his recklessness.

'Cal, don't . . . please,' she begged, clinging to
his arm.

'You will read what is on the paper and those are
the only words you will say,' ordered the man,
punching out a number on the phone. 'Monsieur
de Perregaux?' he asked into the mouthpiece, then
handed it to Cal. 'Remember—just what's on the
paper,' he warned.

'Jean-Pierre? What are they asking you to do . . .'
As the receiver was snatched from him, the other
two men stepped in—one holding the defiant
Frenchman by his arms while the other began beating him with silent ferocity.

'No!' screamed Jackie, flinging herself between
Cal and his assailant. 'No!'

She was still screaming for them to stop when the
second of the blows she intercepted caught her
across the temple and blotted out the world.

'Jackie, wake up . . . you have to wake up.'
The cool dampness against her face soothed.

'Please, baby, wake up.'

'Don't call me "baby",' she muttered irritably,
then groaned. 'My head . . .'

'Thank God you're awake! You're going to have
one hell of a black eye.'

Her eyes opened and she gave a gasp of horror.
Whatever black eye she might develop, she was
certain nothing could match the one Cal now
sported. His left eye was almost closed, the dark,

puffy swelling surrounding it spreading outward and downward to where it blended with the livid gash across his cheek.

'Cal, what have they done to you?' she choked, dragging herself upright and cupping his battered face in her hands. 'Oh, my poor Cal,' she whispered brokenly, her hands shaking as she gently smoothed back the tousled black hair clinging damply to his forehead.

'How do you feel?' he asked, his words thick and distorted from the swelling of his mouth.

'Just a bit of a headache,' she exclaimed dismissively. 'Cal, what on earth did they do to you?'

'They managed to convince me that it was wiser to read their little script.' He took her by the wrists, removing her hands from his face. 'I've put the washing on to dry—I'll get it.' Having made that incongruously domesticated statement, he rose and left her.

Her eyes followed him, mesmerised by the almost lazy fluidity of his walk, drinking in a sight now so familiar that it was impossible for her mind to take the journey back to the time when that walk, that large, yet uniquely graceful body, had not filled her every waking moment.

Had their paths crossed under normal circumstances, he would have passed her by with no more than a second glance from those flirting grey-green eyes. But their circumstances were not normal. Now their lives were entwined beyond all the bounds of normality—intermingling with almost the same casual intimacy as their clothes that now danced together in the dryer.

And, for reasons she had no strength to examine, tears begun chasing slowly down her cheeks, splashing noiselessly as they fell to her clenched hands.

'Jackie, don't . . . it won't help,' he pleaded quietly, handing her the T-shirt and briefs.

'Ignore me—it'll pass,' she choked, unable to stem the hot, salty flow. She slipped into her clothes, accepting the uncharacteristic tears with an empty, unquestioning fatalism.

'Jackie, there are some things we can't ignore any longer,' he stated uncompromisingly, flinging himself down on his bed. 'I've a feeling that it might not just be money they're after—that my life is the price if they fail.'

'Your life and mine, Cal,' she told him quietly, hugging her knees to her chest as she looked over at him. 'How can that fact be so clear in my mind—yet so uncertain in yours?' she asked sadly.

'Perhaps I find it easier to hope you are a part of them,' he sighed.

'For God's sake—what could they possibly gain by incarcerating one of their own with you?' she demanded angrily. 'They won't even tell *you* what they want, so what use could a stool pigeon be to them?'

'There's no angle you can argue from that I haven't already done so with myself,' he exclaimed. 'Perhaps it is moral cowardice, but now I'd *prefer* it if you were one of them. Jackie, I don't want you to die . . . just because fate crossed our paths.'

'And you're convinced we *are* going to die, aren't you, Cal?' she asked woodenly, the terrible lassitude creeping over her making argument impossible.

'There's no way out of this place. A cat would

have problems getting out by the windows; the walls are solid pre-cast concrete, and the only door is impassable. Our visitors come in twos, if not threes, and they're always armed. Does that answer your question?' he asked, his words spoken in a chilling monotone.

'So . . . what do we do?' whispered Jackie, perspiration trickling between her breasts like clammy fingers of fear as the lassitude left her completely.

'If I think of anything, you'll be the first to know.'

'Will I, Cal?' she asked tonelessly.

'Yes, Jackie, you will,' he sighed.

He made no comment when she rose, taking with her the damp towel with which he had bathed her face.

She went to the bathroom, the sense of loneliness and isolation within her gnawing away at her spirit with its unmitigated constancy as she wrung out the towel in cold water.

He rolled on to his back when she returned and sat down on the edge of his bed.

'Jackie, try to take no notice of me,' he muttered, his eyes lowered from hers as she began gently bathing his damaged face. 'I'm moody at the best of times and this is hardly . . . ouch! Hell, I think they've loosened some of my teeth!' There was an expression of horror on his face as he gingerly ran his tongue over his bottom teeth. 'This one—it's wobbling all over the place,' he exclaimed, opening his mouth for her to examine teeth that were strong and even and gleaming white. 'Feel it,' he ordered, grabbing her hand and pressing her forefinger against a rock-solid tooth. 'God, it's on the verge of dropping out,' he groaned, obviously horrified.

'Stop being so vain,' she grinned, the laughter

bubbling in her miraculously dispersing her feelings of lonely isolation. 'I'd no idea you could be such a great big baby!'

'That reminds me,' he remarked, at once losing interest in the state of his perfect teeth. 'Why did you object to my calling you "baby"?'

Jackie shrugged. 'I don't know . . . I'm just not keen on casual endearments.' Not that he went in for them, she reminded herself sharply. 'Perhaps I've seen too many films—where gangsters always call their molls "baby",' she added, confused by the gentle, almost caressing mockery in the eyes now raised to hers.

'Do you know the thought that entered my mind the first time I saw you?' he asked softly, confusing her further with this abrupt change of subject.

She shook her head, her eyes escaping his.

'I wondered why such a beautiful woman—and you are a very beautiful woman, Jackie—should wear her hair scraped back in so prim and unappealing a fashion . . . almost as though she were trying to disguise that beauty.'

Jackie's eyes widened momentarily. There was a mixture of pain and surprise in the look she gave him, and she sensed he had missed neither.

'Come on,' he coaxed. 'Tell me what I've unintentionally stirred up.'

He missed nothing, she thought uncomfortably, puzzled as to why she should find this so unsettling.

'Nadine always used to tease me when I put my hair up like that,' she stated hesitantly. 'She said I might just as well hang a sign round my neck saying I was being chased by someone in whom I had no interest.'

He chuckled. 'Who was the unwanted admirer in Biarritz?'

Jackie shrugged. 'Just one of the students.' She gave her total concentration to his face, her touch a delicate whisper as she washed the congealed blood from around his gashed cheek. The student had been Henri—the lanky, dark-eyed, brooding boy—the person responsible for the trauma that was now their existence.

'Is there someone to whom you wished to remain faithful in England?' he asked, closing his eyes.

'No—there's no one in England.'

'I aways suspected Englishmen might be blind . . . now I know they are,' he chuckled. 'I wonder if you're photogenic . . . who knows, perhaps I could make a star of you.'

'Who says I'd want to be a star?' she laughed, a laugh that sounded nervous and strained to her ears.

'Isn't that what most beautiful women want . . . and those not so beautiful? Jackie, what do you plan doing, when you're back in England.'

'I was thinking of doing a postgraduate teaching diploma . . .'

'To become a French mistress?' he murmured, deliberately emphasising the double meaning of his words. When he opened his eyes, it was just in time to catch the unguarded mixture of tenderness and exasperation on her face. 'Jackie, we shall get out of this mess,' he promised softly. 'And when we do . . . I think I'm going to miss having you around. Will you miss me?'

'I very much doubt it,' she lied unconvincingly.

'Of course you will,' he chuckled. 'For a start, you won't have anyone to do your washing and drying for you!'

CHAPTER FOUR

'GO TO hell! I'm not interested in any more of your stupid games!'

Jackie clung warningly to Pascal de Perregaux's arm, panicked by the reckless, murderous anger blazing from his eyes at their three captors.

With an exclamation of fury, he shook himself free of her hold.

'Get her out of here!' he shouted.

Jackie felt the colour drain from her face as she saw the madness of the anger in him, blotting out the man who, for the entire day, had been more relaxed than she had ever seen him, leaving her at times weak with laughter with his outrageous tales of the film world. Then the laughter had gone, killed when the familiar sounds of the opening door had brought a moment of deathly silence between them, before his rage had exploded with a force she found far more disturbing then the unwelcome presence of their three visitors.

'Cal, please . . .' she pleaded.

'Get her out!' he yelled, advancing on the silent leader and towering over him. 'I want her out of here.'

A nod of the man's head brought one of the others to Jackie's side. She turned as her arm was taken, her eyes pleading as they clung to the tall, unyielding figure of the Frenchman, his back towards her.

She heard his angry words begin again, even as she was shoved roughly through the bedroom door. And she threw herself on the bed, sobbing hysterically and pressing her hands against her ears to blot out the terrible sounds now coming from the kitchen. For several minutes she rocked back and forth in an orgy of fear and hopelessness. But it was in the silence that then came that she began to understand the true terrors of fear. It took less than a couple of seconds for the silence to break her—to send her racing back into the kitchen.

Cal was slumped senseless on the floor. The three men were leaving.

'There's really no necessity for this,' stated the thickset man coldly. 'A man of any intelligence would realise he had no option but to do as we ask.' The door swung closed behind him.

'He's right!' sobbed Jackie, on her knees beside that stubborn, lifeless form, cradling him in her frantic arms. 'Only an utter fool would lose his temper the way you did! Cal, what are you trying to do? Get yourself killed?'

'Go away!' he groaned, as she tried to roll his body over.

'For God's sake, Cal—you must be out of your mind! Get up, damn you!'

'I'm trying to,' he grumbled, then groaned as he sat up.

'Why did you make them send me away?' she sobbed, flinging herself against him. 'They could have been killing you for all I knew! I hate you! I hate your temper—it's going to kill you . . . to kill us both! Cal . . .'

'Jackie, give it a rest, will you?' he muttered irritably, wincing as he placed an arm round her. 'I admit I have a diabolical temper—I've just paid a hefty price for it . . .'

'And what the hell do you think I've been doing?' she sobbed uncontrollably, knowing what a spectacle she was making of herself and hating him for being the cause of it.

'Give me a hand up, will you? I need a shower. And stop crying, for God's sake!' he added harshly.

'What am I supposed to do?' she choked in fury, as the two of them struggled to their feet. 'You're a great comfort to have around,' she continued, her rage only increasing as she followed him into the bathroom. 'You're a selfish pig!' she informed him, not batting an eyelid as he stepped out of his shorts and into the shower. 'Just because you have no control over your temper, we could both be killed!'

'What?' he bellowed over the swoosh of the water.

'I said we could . . . oh, forget it!'

'How about some coffee? he yelled, wincing as he manged a grin. 'You could make a compromise—twice as strong as you like it and half as strong as I do.'

'Thay way, neither of us will be satisfied.'

'What?'

'That way . . I hate you, Cal de Perregaux, do you know that? I honestly hate you!' She picked up a towel and buried her face in it, sobbing with the abandon of a small child in the midst of an uncontrollable tantrum.

'Hey—what's all this about?' whispered a puzzled voice beside her. Dripping arms enfolded her against an equally dripping body, soaking her flimsy clothing. 'This isn't like you, baby . . .'

'Don't call me "baby"!' she shrieked. 'And why isn't this like me? You don't know anything about me! You're too busy throwing your tantrums to care how I might feel! You obviously have no idea what it was like for me—listening to you shouting at them—then hearing what they were doing to you. Not knowing . . . just imagining . . .'

'Jackie, I'm sorry. I should have thought . . .'

'But you didn't!' she accused, shoving him from her. 'But why should you? You believe I'm one of them half the time!'

'Jackie, I'm sorry for putting you through this,' he said quietly, his eyes worried as he knotted a towel round his waist. 'Come on, I'll make the coffee your way.'

'You're even too stupid to work that out,' she rounded on him viciously. 'All you have to do is make it your way and boil extra water to dilute mine!'

'My, a budding genius,' he drawled. 'How come it took so long for you to figure it out?' For an instant his face held its scowling expression, then it was transformed by an angelic, if somewhat lop-sided, smile.

'I bet that hurt,' she gloated, refusing to be mollified.

'You've no idea how much,' he murmured, immediately giving a groan of exasperation as her eyes softened and filled with tears once again. 'For God's sake, Jackie!' he exclaimed in disgust.

'If you think I'm enjoying this, you're mistaken,' she informed him through clenched teeth and tears. 'It's irritating me every bit as much as it is you . . . so much so that I can't even enjoy the fact that it's irritating you!' Realising there was little in the way of dignity left for her to muster, she turned on her heel and marched out.

'Stop following me!' she snapped as he shadowed in her footsteps. 'It's like having a dirty great dog at my heels.'

'I intend making sure you use enough coffee,' he informed her coldly. 'And I don't like being referred to as a dog,' he added in an even more frigid tone.

'I'll refer to you as I like—and you can damn well make the coffee yourself, as you're such a perfectionist!'

He did so—slamming around and making as much mess as he possibly could, while Jackie put on extra water to boil.

'Poetic justice demands that we get out of this place,' he snarled, ladling twice as much coffee as even he required into the filter. 'Because the film I intend making of this little episode is going to be the blackest comedy of all time!'

'Surely you mean kitchen-sink drama—*baby,*' she drawled, in the infuriating tone he often used, as she pointedly handed him a cloth.

'What's this for?'

'To clear up the mess you're having such fun making.'

He flung the cloth at her, scowling.

'Temper, temper,' she murmured, hurling it back.

'Jacqueline, I'm sure I can't possibly be the first to point this out to you, but you are an out and out bitch!'

'Why, because I'm not about to clear up the mess you're making?' she demanded. 'I'm obviously not as stupid as the women you usually come across.'

'Just keep talking,' he snarled. 'I'm storing it all in my head—for the script.'

'Oh, yes—you could produce and direct it too, and star in it. In fact, all you'd have to do to turn it into a one-man show would be to play us both—you'd look great in drag!'

As she spoke, he began coughing. At first it sounded like the rumble of fury in him, then it became a definite cough. The next thing she knew, he was sprawled over the sink, being violently sick.

'Cal!' she screamed in pure terror, her hands shaking uncontrollably as she turned on the taps and began splashing cold water on his ashen face. 'Cal, I swear I didn't mean any of those things . . .'

'Jackie, just shut up, will you?' he groaned, startling her by slipping an arm round her. 'I didn't mean any of it, either,' he told her brusquely.

Knowing she was giving a pretty good imitation of a demented mother hen, and unable to do anything about it, she followed his staggering steps into the bathroom.

'Cal, please . . . you should be lying down.'

'I've got to brush my teeth,' he muttered, then frowned. 'Hell, I forgot—we've only the one brush.'

She squeezed a ribbon of toothpaste on the brush and handed it to him.

'Are you sure?'

'If you like, I'll brush them for you,' she offered, trying desperately to sound humorous while meaning every word. With a scowl, he took the brush from her.

'Do you think it was something you ate?' she asked, knowing her fussing would irritate him beyond all measure, yet unable to curb it. 'Mine tasted OK.'

She waited in hovering attendance as he spent a good five minutes brushing his teeth.

'It's nothing to do with anything I've eaten,' he muttered, pushing his way past her and entering the bedroom. 'My stomach obviously doesn't take too kindly to being used as a punchbag,' he added tartly, flinging himself down on the bed and burying his face in the pillow.

'Cal, shall I get you something? Could you manage some coffee—or perhaps you'd prefer water?'

'Coffee.'

'Water might be better for you . . .'

'Why the hell did you ask, then?'

'All right—I'll get you coffee,' she told him quietly, her mind preoccupied by the unquestionable fact that worry over him now had her in a state verging on total panic.

She was beginning to lose track of the days, she fretted, her trembling hands slopping coffee everywhere as she poured it. But, however many they were, they were enough to have turned a complete stranger into the central pivot of her life.

She had to pull herself together, she chanted silently. He was right—his body had reacted in a perfectly understandable way to the terrible pounding it had taken . . . nothing more. She carried the two mugs of coffee into the bedroom, determined to behave like the rational human being she was.

'Oh my God!' she wailed, managing to deposit the mugs on the floor before they fell from her weakening hands. 'Cal!' she pleaded, frantically shaking the inert figure on the bed.

'What?' he groaned, glowering in protest as he sat up.

'I . . . I thought you were dead . . .'

'It's a wonder I'm not, with you heaving me around like that! For God's sake, Jackie, stop behaving like a complete neurotic—you're making me nervous!'

She sat on the edge of the bed, the knuckles of her clenching, twisting fingers stark white against the tan of her hands. 'Cal, I'm fully aware of the way I'm behaving—it's making me cringe.' She gave a sigh of pure frustration. 'But no matter how hard I try, there's no way I seem able to stop it . . . I've never felt so . . . so completely out of control of my reactions.'

He put out a restraining hand as she remembered the coffee and stooped to retrieve the mugs.

'I'll get it,' he murmured with a wry smile. 'The idea of hot coffee being slopped over me doesn't hold much appeal.' The smile deepened as he passed her a mug. 'Grab it tightly,' he warned. She did so, taking several gulps of the drink, her eyes glued to the floor as she felt his fingers reach out and stroke her cheek. 'Jackie, I owe you an explanation,' he told her quietly. 'Perhaps I should have realised the terrible uncertainty for you—not knowing what they might be doing to me. But I couldn't trust you . . .'

'No!' she exclaimed bitterly, brushing his hand aside. 'You couldn't trust me! You've never trusted me!'

'I couldn't trust you not to do something stupid again,' he continued softly. 'When they did this to you,' his fingers returned to her cheek, gently tracing the bruising around her eye, 'I wanted to kill them. Jackie, the only reason I didn't want you present was because, if they'd touched you again, I knew I'd quite likely go berserk.'

For a reason that had no logical explanation, she wanted to grab the hand on her cheek and cover it with kisses. She restrained herself only with considerable difficulty.

'Jackie, I know my weaknesses—and one of them is my temper. My mother swears that if she'd had me first, instead of my brother Jean-Pierre, she'd never have had another child. He's very placid, whereas I was displaying the de Perregaux temper from almost the moment I was born.'

'What a terrible thing for your mother to say,' protested Jackie, unwilling to examine the strange feeling of contentment now seeping through her.

'My mother adores me—warts and all. Though she's not nearly as maternal as you can be.'

Jackie drained her mug, aware that she was being mocked and frantically searching her mind for a cutting retort. She was still searching when he lay back and unsuccessfully tried to stifle the groan that escaped him. She leapt up and took the pillow from her own bed.

'Come on,' she stated briskly. 'Let's get you comfortable.'

Resolutely avoiding those mocking eyes, she plumped up both pillows and placed them behind him.

'Just like a little mother,' he murmured, closing his eyes.

'Cal, is there anything I can get you? Anything I can do?' she asked, her eyes recoiling from the ugly welts and bruising appearing on his body.

His eyes opened, the darkness of pain no longer

masked from them. 'All I want is to sleep.' His eyes drooped, then closed once more. 'To sleep in the comfort of your arms,' he muttered drowsily.

'Oh, Cal, you big idiot,' sighed Jackie, no hesitation in her as she sat down, swinging her legs up beside him as she propped her back against the pillows, then slid her arm round his shoulders. He gave an incoherent murmur as he turned, his arm curving across her midriff as his head settled against her. Within minutes his breathing had drifted into the slow, imperceptible rhythm of sleep, where each breath was no more than a gentle whisper of heat against the thin cotton of her top.

Conscious of the ramrod tension in every muscle of her body, she tried to relax. She succeeded for an instant, immediately tensing once more as she found her fingers caressing their way through the tousled darkness of his hair.

She tried steering her mind elsewhere. It took her back to the very first time she had seen him— fleetingly in the hotel lobby. Then she had had no idea who the tall, laughing man was, but she had noticed him just as had every other woman present.

'That's Pascal de Perregaux, the film director,' the girl beside her had sighed. 'Isn't he just the dishiest thing you've ever laid eyes on?'

She had no idea why that, of all thoughts, had come to her mind, but a small smile hovered on her lips as she gazed down at that large body now sprawled against hers. Yes, he probably was the dishiest thing she had ever laid eyes on, this parodoxically intimate stranger asleep in her arms.

The smile remained there, imprinted on her lips as her eyes closed and her head began to droop in sleep.

* * *

When she awoke, only the eerie light, from what must have been an almost full moon, kept the room from complete darkness. And she woke only because the warmth against her had stirred, burrowing softly against her breasts.

'Cal, how do you feel?' she asked, sensing he was awake, but finding her words distorted by the violent shiver of excitement leaping through her as his hands impatiently lifted her T-shirt, allowing his face to nestle against her flesh.

'I feel like the condemned man who has just found paradise,' he breathed, his mouth a hot, enveloping moistness on her breast. 'Take this off,' he urged, tugging at the top, then quickly slipping it from her acquiescent body. 'Now these,' he whispered softly, his mouth still wreaking its plundering excitement on her flesh as his hands, swift and sure, swept the briefs from her trembling body. 'I want the magic of you, naked in my arms,' he groaned, casting the towel from around him and drawing her to him. Then his arms tightened, his sharp cry of desire echoed by the softness of hers as he brought her body against the heated arousal of his. For an instant his arms slackened, as though offering her escape, should she wish, from the naked hunger of his desire. But her need was not escape, but to drown in the heady excitement of him. And she felt his arms tighten once more as she silently told him of her need, her body melting with a guileless wholeheartedness against the unyielding strength of his, while her arms wound round him, drawing his mouth to hers to feast and explore in passionate hunger.

Then his hands and his lips were on her body, punishing it with the exquisite torture of their probing touch till all she could do was beg him to stop. And when he heeded her there was a sob of protest on her lips as she berated him, while her body began moving against his in a message of blatant seduction.

'Jackie, you give me no chance to temper my impatience,' he groaned softly, rolling their bodies as the words tumbled from him, till his was poised in tense waiting above hers.

'I don't want you to,' she moaned softly, her hands clinging at his shoulders, drawing him to her. 'Oh, Cal, all I want is your impatient loving,' she pleaded, her body automatically obeying the firm guidance of his with no thought of fear, with no thought save the exciting promise of the virile body hovering on hers.

'Be still, my sweet wildcat,' he gasped, his hands lifting her to receive him. 'Don't be afraid!' he cried out in that moment of sweet, savage pain that was their union.

And her body answered his cry, dispelling the fear that had been in it as an exquisite madness possessed her, burning, then melting, then exploding within her; carrying her above ever-increasing peaks of shuddering sensation till the madness within her spread into him.

'How could I ever be afraid?' she sobbed, drowning in the increasing abandon of his passion, clinging and crying out his name as that passion swelled to a shuddering, violent explosion that swamped her every sense, bombarding her with wave after wave of undreamed-of rapture till she lay spent and gasping in his arms.

'I didn't know,' she choked, her words scarcely audible as her lungs struggled for air. 'How could I have known?' She clung mindlessly to the glistening, still-shuddering body that had taken her beyonds the realms of fantasy.

He moved, easing his weight from her, his arms all the while keeping her trembling body their prisoner. Then he began placing small, panting kisses all over her face.

'Cal, say something—please!' she begged softly, her senses still trapped in wonderment as her lips frantically imitated his.

'When I've recovered.' His attempted laugh was no more than a hoarse gasp. 'When I've recovered—I'll have plenty to say,' he breathed, easing their bodies till hers lay on his.

She lay against him, listening to the thunder of his heartbeat beneath her ear, her hands moving to his shoulders, revelling in the powerful contours they explored, then moving upwards for her fingers to trace the outline of his face.

'I'm checking you, Cal,' she whispered, her tone slightly bewildered.

'Why are you checking me?' he murmured lazily, his breathing now subsided to a less frantic rhythm as his hands began tracing delicate patterns on the small of her back.

'I'm checking to make sure you exist. Because I can't believe what's just happened—that anyone could have the power to make me feel like that . . .'

'Like what?'

'Like . . . how can you ask?' she demanded, uncertainty creeping to her face as she rose to gaze down at him. 'Cal, you must know what I mean. It couldn't be possible for me to feel like that, if you didn't, too . . . it couldn't.'

His answer was a silent shake of his head, but the soft beauty of enchantment had already been stripped from her.

'It could!' she groaned, flinging herself from him and turning on to her side as a terrible emptiness engulfed her. 'I should have warned you I was completely without experience,' she exclaimed bitterly, her naïve words of moments before returning to mock her as her enchantment was swept away on a tidal wave of humiliation.

'Jackie, come back here,' he whispered, his body curving to hers.

'Go away! And don't feel obliged to say anything . . . it's too late, anyway!'

In her eagerness to escape him, she would have fallen off the edge of the bed had he not grabbed her and returned her to her former position on top of him.

'Just you stay put,' he ordered, then added softly, 'There is such a thing as being at a loss for words.'

'Not for you, there isn't,' she retorted, hurt goading her to retaliate where silence would have been wiser. 'You're the first to find words to voice his displeasure.

She stiffened in anger at his soft chuckle.

'But we happen to be discussing my pleasure.' He took her by the shoulders, raising her till there was nowhere for her to look but into his shadowed, enigmatic face. 'And it's my pleasure in you, my sweet Jackie, that leaves me without adequate words.'

'Cal . . . I don't believe you,' she whispered, a sudden and almost suffocating tightness in her chest telling her she lied.

'Jackie, could you find the words to describe what's just happened between us?' he asked huskily, his hands gentle as they stroked aside the curtain of hair falling around her face.

'No, but . . .'

He shook his head. 'No, *because*. Because there are no words.'

'Oh, Cal . . .' She hesitated, savouring the return of enchantment. 'It is always like that?' she asked tremulously, contentment in the hands that returned to exploring his face.

'Jackie, if it were always like that I'd not be at a loss for words.'

She gave an involuntary shiver as a vivid picture of his body, locked in passion with someone other than herself, leapt into her mind. Startled and disturbed, she blurted out the first words that came to her. 'How many times has it been like that?' She winced as he gave a groaning laugh. How could she possibly have asked such a question?

'Jackie, what appalling etiquette . . . you really shouldn't ask questions like that. But the answer is never.'

'I know I shouldn't have asked,' she cried, flinging herself against him while her arms almost throttled him. 'But I'm glad the answer is never!'

'And why are you this glad?' he protested, freeing himself.

'Because . . . it's not that I'd begrudge you enjoying all those before . . .'

'All those?' he groaned in laughing disbelief. 'Jackie, I'm not a callow youth bedding every woman in sight . . . my attitude to sex is far from casual.'

She gave a yelp of indignation as he tugged her

by the hair.

'Jackie, why did you lie to me? Why did you speak of having been on the pill—allowing me to think you were a sexually experienced woman?'

'Cal, I didn't lie—at least, I didn't mean to,' she protested, then explained.

'But you must have realised the inevitability of my conclusions.'

She nodded, her expression one of discomfort. 'I felt a bit embarrassed . . . at the thought of having to explain all that,' she muttered, 'a bit embarrassed' being a gross understatement of how she now felt.

'But you don't feel like that with me now, do you?' he asked softly.

'Yes, I do! Cal, every time I open my mouth I seem to come out with some ghastly gaffe! I wasn't trying to imply you were a womaniser and I certainly wasn't trying to pry into your past. All I was trying to do was to express a fraction of what I'd felt.'

He drew her head down to him, cradling it to the curve of his neck.

'You've made no gaffe, sweet Jackie,' he murmured huskily, the delicate play of his hands against her bringing an excited awareness to her. 'You've just learned that there are some things to which words cannot do justice.'

Her mouth moved against him, her lips parting to taste the salty tang of his skin. Then her mouth moved up further, a soft sigh escaping her as he rediscovered the firm fullness of his lips. Then it was no longer sighs that spilled from her, but soft moans of delight as his hands found her breasts, their tantalising touch rekindling with a savage urgency the fires so recently extinguished in her.

'This is a physical impossibility,' he groaned, while his body gave instant lie to his words with its swift and powerful manifestation of desire.

This time he used strength of both mind and body to tame the passion he ignited, gentling her abandon with the soft coaxing of his words. Then she found words of her own—words that eventually destroyed his control and drove him to take her with him beyond the bounds of reality, to hover and linger in realms of exquisite ecstasy till their passion became an explosion of release that left them floating in the sweetness of oblivion.

She tried to rationalise the hunger that grew within her for him with each passing moment. She tried to blank that hunger from her eyes, knowing it must frighten him, just as it did her.

Yet she knew he sensed it. Often he would reach wordlessly for her, knowing his touch was all it took to ignite the white heat of passion between them. And she found herself wondering how he might react were she ever to feel the need to reach out to him. Then she consoled herself, accepting that the frequency of his desire spoke of a hunger every bit as insatiable as her own.

But the sadness that always came to her after their lovemaking, which she had at first accepted as the only logical emotion to follow the rapturous escape their bodies brought them, now seemed to stay with her for increasingly longer periods.

'Jackie?'

She stirred in his arms as her whispered name broke through that sadness.

'The chances of your becoming pregnant are

more a probability than a possibility now.'

'Yes.' Her eyes were closed, her cheek rested against the soft abrasiveness of the hairs on his chest. She could feel the beat of his heart beneath her—now a steady, unhurried throb. 'It's a probability I recognised and accepted from the start.'

'In what way accepted?' he asked guardedly.

'Though a child is biologically fifty per cent of his father—there are often times when he is one hundred per cent his mother's responsibility.'

'And you would regard a child of ours as that—one hundred per cent your reponsibility?'

There was something in his tone she found unsettling—nothing she could actually pinpoint. She sat up, hugging her knees to her.

'If that's the way things turn out—yes. I'd accept that responsiblity without regrets. Cal, that probably sounds horribly twee and noble . . .' She sighed. 'I think I'm just beginning to understand yet another facet of what being a woman entails.'

'And you resent it?'

'No—I don't resent it!' she exclaimed, his total remoteness setting her nerves on edge. 'I'm merely stating what I see as facts.'

'And what about abortion—would that be a part of the facts?'

Those toneless words ripped through her, chilling the blood in her veins, seeming to condemn any life that might be within her even before its presence could be guaranteed.

'That would be my business,' she snapped, leaping up in her sudden need to escape the threat she found in those words.

He caught her by the wrist, halting her. 'And

you don't consider it might be mine?' he asked chillingly.

She looked down at him—the man whose hot-blooded passion might well have filled her with his child—and saw only the cold arroganace of the stranger he might still have been had fate not so irrevocably entwined their lives.

'No, Cal, I don't.'

CHAPTER FIVE

'HENRI!' gasped Jackie, her entire body freezing with shock. 'I know it's you despite that horrid mask—I know it's you!' She had woken early and gone into the kitchen for a glass of water, only to find the inescapably familiar lanky figure placing the day's groceries on the floor. 'Please, Henri . . .'

'Don't call me by my name,' he rasped, his barely visible eyes glancing nervously towards the door. 'If they heard you, they'd kill you. Why do you think they go to the trouble of always keeping their faces hidden?'

'Who are they?' she begged, all colour draining from her face.

The youth took a step towards her, then hesitated. 'I didn't think they'd bring you, too,' he blurted out. 'I never meant you to come to any harm.'

'I believe you,' she sighed, with an irrational stab of pity. That he was in a state verging on emotional disintegration was all too apparent. His movements were jerky and badly co-ordinated as he stepped nervously back to the door and peered into the unknown darkness beyond it. Then he faced her again, his body almost quivering with pent-up tension.

'They killed someone . . . just shot him dead,' he muttered. 'Just as they'll kill you. No! I can't let them!'

'Henri——' she pleaded, terrified one of the others might join them.

'Don't . . . don't use my name. No one must know that you've recognised me . . . especially not the film man, de Perregaux . . . he doesn't trust you—they know that . . . he's made it obvious. If you tell him of me, he'll let them know . . .'

'Of course he won't,' chided Jackie, alarmed by his obvious mental instability and struggling to overcome her mounting terror in an effort to calm him.

'Swear you'll not tell him,' he begged. 'Then I'll help you—help you both. But only if you swear.'

'I swear—I'll not tell him, I swear,' croaked Jackie, wondering if she had truly lost her mind, as pity for this pathetic creature welled up in her again.

'Just remember—if you mention me to him, the chances are I'll not live to help you,' he repeated, his hoarse intensity sending shivers through her. 'I'll be back tomorrow morning . . . swear you won't tell de Perregaux.'

'I swear,' echoed Jackie, her voice a strangled croak.

Then the door closed behind him and she was alone. She began putting the things away, her hands trembling to such an extent that she dropped items several times.

'I'll make the coffee.'

With a nervous start she clapped her hand to her mouth to silence her cry of fright as she heard Cal's voice from the doorway.

'That's OK, I'll do it,' she managed, picking up the coffee-jug. 'You have your shower.'

'Jackie?'

'Yes.'

'Is there anything you wish to say?'

For an instant her mind froze, filled with Henri's frantic words of warning, before reason returned to her. Bitter anger welled in her as she realised that his words could refer only to the subject that had seemed to obsess him ever since her adamant refusal to discuss it further—her attitude to an abortion should she be pregnant. It had created an insurmountable barrier between them—one that had turned them once more into warring strangers.

'No, Cal. There's nothing I wish to say.'

It had killed everything between them, she realised miserably, her body even now aching with a terrible need.

'Cal, we can't go on like this!' she blurted out.

'You've thought of a way of escape, have you?' he drawled, deliberately misunderstanding her meaning.

Her face was tense and withdrawn as she silently prepared breakfast while all the while a battle raged within her. She was being held prisoner by a gang of thugs—killers, because she had no doubt Henri's words had been the truth—yet the subject preoccupying her, almost to the exclusion of all else, was the sudden and total disintegration of her relationship with Cal. She should be grateful her mind had found something to distract her from the hopelessness of reality, she told herself sharply—it was the sign of a healthy mind. And besides, there was a glimmer of hope, however elusive and unreliable.

She turned to face him, deciding to renege on her oath to Henri and let him share that minute hope. It was his eyes that silenced her, eyes for a moment unguarded in their glittering antagonism before the shutters swiftly descended to conceal what she was seeing.

'I suppose the intelligent thing would be for us to call a truce,' he intoned, as they settled on the floor with their breakfast. 'We each steer clear of topics the other doesn't wish to discuss.'

'And are we going to do the intelligent thing?' asked Jackie, her eyes on the bread he so liberally buttered while her mind still saw what she had glimpsed in those eyes.

He shrugged, then dunked the bread in his coffee. 'We can both claim to be intelligent, can't we?'

Jackie watched the pool of grease forming on the surface of the coffee, the sight dredging up memories of Nadine's surprise on learning from her disapproving niece that the British would consider such eating habits unacceptable.

'Yes, we can,' she sighed, lost in the vividness of her memories.

'I had an English girlfriend once,' he announced out of the blue, and grinned. 'She said watching me eat breakfast left her feeling queasy for the rest of the day. Odd—the English,' he added, dunking his bread once more.

'It surprised me the first time I saw Nadine do it,' murmured Jackie, thrown by his apparent reading of her thoughts. 'This English girl—how long did you live with her?' She felt a flash of panic wing through her as it dawned on her what she had said.

'I didn't—I was a guest at her parents' house for a couple of weeks while I was filming in England . . . she lived at home,' he drawled, making not the slightest effort to conceal his obvious amusement. 'Why? Does it make you feel jealous, Jackie, the thought of me making love with another woman?'

'No, it damn well doesn't!' she retorted, far too hastily. 'It's just that something's been puzzling me.'

'Really?'

'You claim not to have a casual attitude to sex—yet you were propositioning me sexually from the word go.'

'It's a very easy way for a man to intimidate a woman, and I felt a need to intimidate you. Had you done the sensible thing and called my bluff, I'd no doubt have found another way of bullying you.'

'What a charming person you are,' she muttered in disgust.

'Some would say I was merely displaying healthy survival instincts—all being fair in love and war.'

That was the first of several instances of his goading sarcasm, which continued through the day. Not that he was straightforwardly unpleasant—instead he played her much as a skilled angler might, at times sweet and cajoling, at others brusque and unapproachable.

At no time did he reach out to her physically, and it was her reaction to that which disturbed her most of all. Time and again she had silently willed him to do just that, she thought in horror, as she stepped from the shower and dried herself. She sat on the bathroom floor for a long while, trying to sort out her devastated mind, before she eventually rose and went to the bedroom.

He was sprawled on his bed, his hands clasped behind his head, his eyes closed.

'You'll end up with skin like a prune if you keep

showering for hours at a stretch like that,' he muttered.

She stood between the beds and looked down at him, fatalistically accepting the shivers of longing searing through her at the sight of that magnificent golden body.

'And it's a fallacy about cold showers, isn't it, Jackie? They don't help,' he added suddenly, his eyes opening to gaze mockingly into hers.

'No, Cal, they don't,' she replied wearily.

She heard the sharp intake of his breath and saw the mockery darken from his eyes as he suddenly turned over and lay on his stomach.

'You say that with an acceptance I find curious,' he said, his eyes still on hers. 'Doesn't it trouble you—a *nice* girl like you—wanting me as you do?'

'No, it doesn't trouble me in the least,' she replied evenly. 'Fortunately, I happen to possess a fairly rational mind.'

'And you've managed to rationalise the desire you're experiencing?'

'The desire we both feel,' she retorted sharply. 'You and I are in the same boat, Cal.' She made an effort to control her anger. 'I am twenty-four years old, and until a few days ago I was a virgin . . . Cal, why have you closed your eyes?' she taunted softly. His eyes opened, but there was decided wariness in them. 'I didn't consciously hang on to my virginity, and I certainly didn't regard it as a prize to be given out to the worthiest applicant . . .'

'I'm glad to hear that, as you could hardly consider me a worthy applicant,' he drawled.

'How right you are,' she snapped, discovering that it was possible to want and hate at the same moment and with equal intensity. 'If we'd been stranded here for some mundane reason, you and I would never have made love. But I understand now why sex is recognised as the strongest drive of all—it's like a drug that can blot out even the ultimate fear—that of death. Lovemaking was all you and I had as an escape from our fears. I regard the reaction of my body to you as a favour—it's probably the only thing that's allowed me to hang on to my sanity.' Her shoulders straightened slightly. 'And I feel no shame—none whatsoever. Circumstances drove us to . . . I suppose the only word is to "use" one another.'

'*Bravo,* Jackie! I can only offer you my admiration for your words.'

There was no mockery in his eyes—what she saw in them looked curiously like sadness. She turned away, knowing she must be mistaken, and was halted by the hand that reached for hers.

'But you haven't given in to it completely, have you, Jackie?' he asked softly. 'Each time you wanted me, I saw the battle you fought with yourself . . . with me . . . each time you won, and I lost.'

'As I'm being honest, I might as well admit that I'd lost the battle, when I came in here just now.' She hesitated, the hint of a smile creeping to her lips. 'At least, I thought I had, till you made it a draw.'

'A draw?' he queried, his hand urging her towards him. 'Jackie, is it my imagination, or are you blushing?' he whispered, a grin of delight transforming his face. 'Tell me—what changed it to a draw?'

'When you turned over on to your stomach . . . I realised that perhaps you had something to hide.'

He was chuckling as he swept her into his arms.

But there was an almost ferocious intensity to their lovemaking, as though each were trying to erase the memory of those hours apart in the wild abandon of the ecstasy they created in one another time and again.

'There's a part of me that would gladly die in your arms,' he vowed, lying against her once more passion-spent as the ghostly fingers of dawn began folding back the night. 'A primitive part of me that's no longer governed by social or moral strictures.'

Her arms tightened round him, their hold almost protective. 'Circumstances just happen to have placed us temporarily beyond the rules,' she whispered, stroking his hair. 'But I doubt if there's much chance of you dying in my arms,' she added teasingly.

'I'd say there's every chance of it—if we continue to carry on like this,' he chuckled, a drowsy chuckle that was already drifting into sleep.

She had been pacing up and down for almost half an hour before Henri arrived. He was noticeably calmer than he had been the day before, and it was that calmness which gave life to the seed of hope struggling within her.

'It's OK—I'm alone,' he told her, placing the grocery carton on the sink-top. 'You must listen very carefully to everything I say.' Even the eyes behind the mask had a comforting alertness, and the whispered words were firm. 'De Perregaux's brother isn't co-operating . . . they're going to contact him once more.' He placed a hand on her shoulder. 'They're getting desperate . . . and killing you both would come easily to them,' he added in a strangely gentle voice that made Jackie's blood run cold. 'I don't intend letting that happen. Jackie, at seven this evening that door will be unlocked.'

'But it can't be opened from this side,' she blurted. 'There's no handle . . .'

'Ease something down the edge, it will swing open easily.'

'Where does it lead to?' she babbled, making a conscious effort to control herself as every part of her began shaking.

'Just into a passageway between here and the main building. There's a door to the left of this, which leads to the garden. That, too, will be unlocked tonight.'

Jackie leaned heavily against the sink, trying to take in his words while her mind obstinately refused to function.

'Henri, will you be there?' she choked eventually.

'No. But you follow the path right through the garden. At the end there's a small gate—I can't unlock that, so you'll have to climb over it.'

'Henri . . .'

'Listen . . . please! There will be a motorbike to the left of the gate, against the hedge—the keys will be in it.'

'But, Henri . . .'

'Please,' he begged. 'Just listen, I haven't much time. Donnier, the guy in charge—and two of his henchmen—have gone off somewhere. They're not due back till later, but I don't know how late. Jackie, you're not to tell de Perregaux until the very last minute.' He held up a silencing hand as she tried again to speak. 'You can't blame him for not trusting you, but you must keep it in your mind that he doesn't.'

'But he wants to get away from here every bit as much as I do!' she protested. It was the terrible intensity of the sudden tension in him that frightened her, silencing her protest. 'Henri, I'll do exactly what you ask—I promise.'

Though he tried to contain it, she was conscious of that brittle tension now racking him as he made her repeat his instructions. 'Just remember—remember everything I've said. *Adieu, Jackie,*' he whispered quietly. Then he was gone.

She wanted to call him back—perhaps to thank him—perhaps to ask some of the questions flooding into her mind, but he was gone. She put the food away, going over and over his instructions as she tried to calm herself, busying herself, doing everything in her power to contain the fear and hope that raged in battle within her.

She had made coffee and was just smoothing out the clothes she had put through the dryer in an effort to get rid of some of their creases, when Cal appeared in the doorway.

'The guard's been,' he observed, and began pouring coffee. 'Want some?'

Jackie nodded, wondering if he would comment on the clothes she was sorting—his shirt and jeans, her skirt—clothes they had not worn since their arrival. And as she wondered she was torn by the mixture of emotions the sight of him stirred in her; half of her welcoming the distraction of his presence, while the rest of her dreaded what she might give away.

'Would you like some bread?' he asked politely.

Again she nodded, trying to equate those formal tones with the voice that had filled her ears almost throughout the night, sometimes husky with endearment, at others harsh in its cries of passion.

'You look almost as worn out as I feel,' he remarked when they had finished breakfast, his words a simple statement that contained no edge of either sarcasm of humour. 'I'm going to shower, and then get some sleep.' He rose, his face expressionless as he looked down at her. 'Perhaps you should get some sleep, too.'

There was no perhaps about it, she told herself. Plenty of sleep was what they would both need if they were to have their wits about them for the night ahead. But she found sleep impossible. It both amazed and relieved her that it should come to him so easily. Twice during the day, when she heard him get up, she had to feign sleep as she heard him leave the room. She listened to him pad around, then to the sound of him showering; again feigning sleep when he eventually returned and lay down, envying him the gentle evenness of his breathing as he again slipped into the refuge of the sleep denied her.

'Try to eat some of it,' she coaxed as she watched him toy half-heartedly with the meal she had prepared.

'Why?' he demanded rudely.

'For heaven's sake!' she snapped. 'We missed lunch—I thought you'd want your supper early.' She should have just told him, she thought distractedly, she would have to any moment now.

He shrugged, then began eating.

'Cal, have you seen our shoes at all?' she asked suddenly.

'We arrived here barefoot—perhaps there's a

local taboo against footwear,' he stated, his eyes shrewd as they caught and held hers.

Jackie's gaze dropped from his and on to her watch. Her heart was pounding and her mouth had gone completely dry. It was almost seven and she could no longer put off telling him. Her eyes rose to his once more and the antagonism she found there snapped something in her. She could forgive—even understand—his original lack of trust in her. What she could never forgive was the distrust he still felt—even now—after all that had happened between them.

She rose, cold determination in her as she went over to the folded clothes on top of the dryer and handed him his.

'Put these on, you'll need them—we're getting out of here,' she ordered, and stepped into her skirt.

'You don't say,' he drawled, his eyes glittering their hostility as he dressed. 'And where exactly are we going?'

'Just shut up and follow me,' she rasped, fear a palpitating presence throughout her as she glanced at her watch and picked up a fork.

'Arming yourself?' he enquired with cold venom.

Jackie scarcely heard the words, desperately trying to still the violent shaking of her hand as she eased the prongs of the fork down the side of the door. Dear God, what if it didn't work? It slid open effortlessly.

'Hurry!' she urged, then felt panic flood through her as she stepped into complete darkness.

Remembering Henri's words, she groped along the wall to the left of her, her knees almost buckling with her relief as she found a handle and wrenched open the door.

The path was long, seemingly unending, and its gravelled sharpness was painful beneath her bare, racing feet.

'We'll have to climb this,' she panted when they eventually reached the padlocked gate.

Without a word he lifted her over, then leapt across himself. The motorbike was exactly where Henri had said it would be.

'You can ride one of these, can't you?' she begged, the thought that he couldn't suddenly turning to certainty in her beleaguered mind.

He straightened the huge machine and straddled it, impatiently motioning her to get on behind him. She gave a sob of fright, burying her face against his back as the powerful machine roared to life, then seemed to lift off into the darkness.

She was waiting for the sound of gunshots to follow them; waiting for the car that would intercept them; waiting, and hating the cowardice within her that now longed for the comparative safety of their prison.

And even when he at last felt it safe to turn on the headlamp and when the kilometres had begun to speed by, that constant and horror-filled waiting refused to leave her, and there was no more than a numb fatalism in her when she felt the bike swerve beneath them, nearly throwing her off, before coming to a halt. They would kill them then and there, she told herself, still clinging to that strong, unyielding back.

'Get off, I need to look in the panniers,' he ordered.

Unable to take in his words, Jackie clung

silently, her body being carried by his as he tried to dismount.

'For God's sake, Jackie, let go—I want to get off!'

She leapt off, unable to believe that they were alone on the deserted road, and watched as he opened the side of the pillion on which she had been sitting.

'I need something—anything—to protect my eyes, I can hardly see.'

Jackie looked into his face in the half-light—his eyes were swollen and streaming.

'Thank God,' he exclaimed, producing a pair of goggles and putting them on. 'We're a few kilometres west of Avignon.' He gave a bitter laugh as he remounted the bike. 'A fact of which you were no doubt well aware. We'll make straight for Paris—away from the toll roads.'

'Wouldn't the toll roads be quicker?' she demanded, his earlier remark drawing no reaction from her—she no longer cared what he thought, she realised, just as long as they made it as far from here as possible and as quickly as possible.

'Marginally—but all I have on me is credit cards,' he snapped, motioning her back on to the bike.

They stopped twice for petrol. On neither occasion did he address so much as a single word to her. When they arrived on the outskirts of Paris, it was more of a sixth sense that told her where they were—the rest of her senses were dulled to a state bordering on comatose. She was frozen and would gladly have slept, however dangerous, had it not been for the gnawing fear that hung on with an indestructible tenacity within her.

'We're here.' His words were shouted, but they held little joy. Perhaps his ears were still filled with the throb of the engine, thought Jackie inconsequentially as she felt herself pulled roughly from the bike.

They were in the middle of Paris, she thought in confusion, yet they were surrounded by immaculately tended lawns—before a house like something out of a soap opera.

She gave a cry of protest as her arm was taken in a painful grasp and she was dragged towards the curved sweep of stone steps leading up to the magnificent house.

'I'm perfectly capable of walking unaided!' she exclaimed, struggling to free herself.

'No doubt. But I'm not letting go of you because I haven't the energy to chase after you should you decide to run,' snarled Cal, his grip tightening with a bruising force.

'What makes you think I'd want to run?' she asked with savage sweetness. 'After all, we've come this far together.'

'If you're banking on the memory of shared passion to soften me—you're wasting your time . . . that's why you'll run, baby.'

'You bastard!' she screamed, taking a vicious swing at him with her free hand and feeling the sharp sting of stubble beneath her palm. 'Of course, you couldn't be wrong, could you, Cal? Not you!' She was kicking in a mad fury at his legs. 'Are all you de Perregaux infallible? Like your precious brother who's too mean to pay for your life!'

This time he caught the hand that had swung back to deal him a second blow, and their struggling bodies were silhouetted in the sudden brightness of light as the large double doors of the house drew open.

'*Mon Dieu! C'est Monsieur Pascal . . . c'est Monsieur Pascal!*'

CHAPTER SIX

THE ELDERLY, dressing-gowned woman who had cried out in such tones of quavering disbelief was gently moved aside by the tall figure of a man.

Jackie's struggles ceased as that man raced down the sweeping stone steps, joy and incredulity battling for supremacy on his handsome features as he wordlessly flung his arms round Cal. There was little doubt in Jackie's mind that this was Jean-Pierre de Perregaux, the brother she had been angrily maligning only seconds before. Though there was a sprinkling of grey in the rich black of the second man's hair and he was a few centimetres shorter, both had the same athletic build, the same remarkably good looks.

'The black sheep has returned,' murmured Cal gently as they hugged, the elder too overcome to speak. 'But there's much to be done before we can celebrate,' he added, freeing himself and turning to Jackie. 'First, we need the police.' His words might have been for his brother, but his bleak expressionless eyes were on Jackie.

'We have a direct line to the police. Madame Genet will be on to them even as we speak. So . . . this is the young lady,' added Jean-Pierre de Perregaux, giving Jackie a small, formal bow.

Jackie was conscious of the puzzlement on Cal's face. 'Yes—but how do you know of her?'

His brother waved a dismissive hand. 'That's for

later. For now, just let me finish convincing myself it's really you!'

Jackie watched, her heart going out to him as he made an effort to bring his emotions under control.

'Perhaps I should wake Marie . . . she's been out of her mind with worry . . . we all have.' He gave a small shudder, then stretched out his hand to Jackie. 'You are most welcome in the de Perregaux home, Miss Templeton,' he told her in faultless English.

'She speaks French, and don't be too sure she's welcome here,' growled Cal, grabbing Jackie by the wrist and yanking her roughly up the steps behind him.

'Cal, what are you saying?' protested his brother, horror in his expression as he accompanied them into a huge marbled hall which, under normal circumstances, might have left Jackie reeling from the sheer opulence of its elegant beauty.

Her eyes dropped unseeingly to the richly patterned rug beneath her bare feet.

'What he's saying is that I'm in league with his kidnappers, whoever they were,' she stated tonelessly. 'You seem to know something of me—so perhaps you can convince him otherwise . . . though I can't say I'm particularly interested in what he or anyone thinks any more.' She knew she was behaving appallingly, and knew she should apologise. But she was having problems with the rug—its pattern kept changing, hurting her eyes as it billowed upwards as though reaching out to her.

'Madame Genet!' bellowed Cal, the loudness of his voice jarring Jackie in the instant he caught her. 'Find her a room and get her to bed.'

Other, far gentler hands took and supported her.

'And get Jacques up—I want him to stand guard outside her room . . .'

'Cal, is that absolutely necessary?' cut in his brother, his tone horrified.

'It's absolutely necessary.'

Jackie felt herself being led from the room, but her head swam uncomfortably each time she attempted to focus on her surroundings. She felt almost agoraphobic, there was so much space around her—graceful, marble-columned space; gold and white elegance gleaming from the shimmering light of chandeliers—space uncluttered in its understated beauty of line, yet rich with opulence even in its understatement.

Despite her reeling head, it registered that Pascal de Perregaux's family home was the nearest thing to a fairy-tale of perfection she had ever seen, and her grogginess was tinged with disbelief as she was led into a spacious room, the predominant colours of which seemed to be blue and white.

'Bedroom' was too plebian a word for such elegance, she decided as she flung her unkempt form on to the silken covers of the large bed and immediately found the lights in her mind switching themselves off.

'Mademoiselle Templeton?'

Jackie emerged from the luxuriously appointed adjoining bathroom to find the housekeeper hovering by the main door.

'Bonjour, madame,' she murmured, smiling uncertainly as she belted the blue towelling robe around her slim body.

'Did you sleep well?' asked Madame Genet, smiling sympathetically as her eyes took in the dark exhaustion beneath the wide-spaced blue eyes.

'Very well,' lied Jackie. She had tossed in fitful wakefulness for the entire night.

'Madame de Perregaux was taken to the clinic two hours ago—the excitement of Monsieur Pascal's returning had started the baby,' confided the housekeeper, her eyes twinkling happily.

'When was the baby due?' asked Jackie in alarm.

'Next week—so it's not too soon,' comforted the woman, noting Jackie's alarm and visibly warming to her. 'Jacques has brought up your luggage—I'll get it for you.'

Jackie looked at her blankly.

'Your things from Biarritz,' explained Madame Genet gently. 'We have them here.'

'That's good news—but I can get them my-self . . .'

'No need, I have them.'

Jackie glanced behind the housekeeper to where Cal de Perregaux stood in the doorway, her suitcase in one hand, her holdall in the other.

'Now, don't you keep her talking, Monsieur Pascal. I'm sure she could do with a good break-fast in her,' fussed the housekeeper, giving Jackie a warm smile as she slipped past the grim-faced man and out.

'I take it Madame Genet has yet to be en-lightened about my being one of the criminal fraternity,' muttered Jackie, opening the case he placed on the dainty gold and walnut dressing-stool and trying to focus her mind on its contents.

'I've said nothing to the police that could implicate you,' he stated woodenly, his gaze concentrated on the highly polished leather of his shoes.

Jackie turned to him, her eyes almost greedy as they drank in the white silk of the shirt that clung and rippled sensuously against his body, its paleness sharply contrasting with the darkness of the close-fitting trousers that skimmed down the long line of his legs.

She hated this man, she told herself fiercely, hated him almost as much as she did herself for the terrible need that lived on in her.

'How very noble of you, Cal,' she replied with a bitterness she could not conceal. 'But the end result of such nobility will be only to make a fool of yourself. I intend telling the police the truth.'

'Forget about the truth—it's a bit late for that,' he snapped, his eyes rising to hers, cold and accusing. 'You'll tell the police no more than you told me. Unfortunately, there were certain stories my brother felt obliged to give the press—and I want my family name protected as far as it can be.'

'Damn your family name!' she cried, loathing the part of her that had foolishly hoped it might be herself he had wanted to protect

'It was your name, too, that concerned my brother,' he informed her coldly.

'My name doesn't need protecting,' she retorted. 'There's no dishonour in being an innocent victim of kidnap and, impossible though you find it to accept, that's all I am!'

'Use your brain,' he exclaimed impatiently. 'When it came to the attention of the press that I was missing, Jean-Pierre was hardly able to tell them the truth, and it didn't take much journalistic snooping to discover that an attractive English girl, staying in the same hotel, was missing, too.'

'Why should anyone notice my absence?' demanded Jackie.

'A girl you had arranged to meet for lunch, the day after we were taken, noticed. She made enquires at the hotel.'

Jackie frowned, struggling to remember—it all seemed a lifetime ago.

'By then my brother had been contacted, and the hotel manager was one of the few people who had been let in on the truth.'

'And what exactly were others told?' asked Jackie.

He gave that familiar dismissive shrug. 'That you and I needed some privacy . . . that soon an announcement would probably be made regarding our forthcoming marriage.'

'Our what?' exclaimed Jackie, and gave a harshly bitter laugh. 'What a romantic brother you have!' Angrily, she began removing clothes from her case.

'As I said, he was trying to protect your name . . . would you like those ironed?'

She gave a shrug of indifference.

'I'll get Madame Genet to have it seen to.' He moved to the door, then turned and faced her. 'My brother asks that you join us for breakfast on the terrace. The police will be here soon to speak to you.'

'And what about you—or have they finished with you?'

'I had a three-hour session with them while you were sleeping—there's little more I can give them—no matter what you choose to say.'

When he had gone, Jackie slipped into a green cotton shift, the least crumpled of her clothes, and a pair of high-heeled sandals. She was free, she kept telling herself as she vigorously brushed her hair in front of a gilt-framed oval mirror. But the reminder brought her no comfort, and she knew she was deliberately putting off the moment she would have to leave the sanctuary of this beautiful room.

A light rap took her to the door, and she found herself blinking in surprise at the sight of a uniformed maid standing before her. 'Madame Genet has asked me to get your ironing,' explained the girl, her eyes wide with curiosity.

'Everything's been folded for so long, I'm afraid it's rather badly creased,' apologised Jackie.

'I'll sort it out for you—just leave it to me,' offered the girl, smiling as Jackie glanced contritely towards the heap of clothes on the bed. '*Monsieur* is waiting for you.'

Jackie nodded, unsure to which *monsieur* the maid was referring. 'I'm sorry, but I don't know my way around—how do I get to the terrace?'

With a friendly laugh, the girl led her to the top of the magnificent marbled staircase and gave her directions. There was an expression of wry disbelief on Jackie's face as she descended the stairs, passing huge, gilt-framed painting after painting of what she guessed must be de Perregaux ancestors. This must be the ultimate in gracious living, she mused as she made her way through spacious luxury and out on to the large terrace overlooking immaculately tended lawns.

Jean-Pierre de Perregaux rose from his seat at an oval, wrought-iron table, and bowed.

'Did you sleep well, Miss Templeton?' he asked, with polite formality.

'Yes, thank you,' she murmured, disconcerted by the alien feelings of gaucherie and shyness overtaking her as she took a seat.

'Please, call me Jackie—Miss Templeton sounds so formal.' She immediately regretted her words and awaited a rebuff. First names were reserved for friends, and Cal had made it quite plain she should be considered an enemy.

'And please call me Jean-Pierre,' smiled the attractive man, so like his brother, yet seeming much gentler and more approachable than the man he resembled.

His eyes, those familiar grey-green eyes, widened in alarm as Jackie gave a sudden gasp.

'Your wife!' she groaned. 'Madame Genet told me . . . how is she?'

Jean-Pierre de Perregaux gave a soft chuckle that sent shivers of recognition winging through her. 'The events of last night were too much for her. She was so happy, it seemed our baby was about to join in the celebrations, but it turned out to be a false alarm.' The smile he gave lent boyish happiness to his face. 'They're keeping her in for a while as the baby's practically due, anyway.'

And the thought obviously delighted him, realised Jackie with the tiniest twinge of envy. She turned as a maid arrived with a laden tray.

'I ordered you boiled eggs,' murmured Jean-Pierre with a touch of uncertainty. 'It must seem like a long time since you last ate.'

'And you couldn't have made a better choice,' smiled Jackie, helping herself to an egg. Then the smile died on her lips as the uncertainty of her status suddenly overwhelmed her. 'Monsieur . . . Jean-Pierre, I wasn't involved with them,' she blurted out in desperation. 'I know Cal is convinced I was . . . but I wasn't, I swear it.'

'Jackie, as far as I am concerned you brought my brother back to me—alive. That's all that interests me, for the time being.'

'But you don't discount the possibility that I might have been involved,' she stated miserably.

'From what information we managed to get on you, I'd say your being involved was most unlikely. But, as you say, my brother seems convinced otherwise,' he added quietly.

'Having met you, there's something that puzzles me,' mused Jackie aloud. 'You obviously love Cal—yet you refused to pay. Did they ask so much even a family as wealthy as yours couldn't afford it?'

'It wasn't a question of money,' he replied, his eyes now shrewd and guarded as she had so often seen his brother's. He hesitated noticeably before continuing, 'Do you know anything of the French judicial system?'

Jackie shook her head.

'Ours differs in many ways from that of Britain. I suppose the nearest comparable position to mine would be that of Attorney General. There is a case coming before our courts next week, which involves an international drug-smuggling ring.'

Those uncomfortably familiar eyes seemed to bore through her as Jackie returned their gaze with complete openness.

'My brother was taken by the remnants of the gang—we have the ringleaders—in the hope that I would be persuaded to have the case dropped. It was a vain hope, there was nothing I could have done even had I wanted to.'

Despite the warmth of the morning sun, Jackie shivered. 'Our deaths would have been inevitable,' she stated faintly.

'They had made the threat.' He shrugged grimly. 'I can't imagine men like that not carrying it out.'

The aftermath of those words was still clouding their faces when Cal and two other men joined them.

'We have three of them,' announced the taller of the two strangers, addressing Jean-Pierre, as Cal flung himself down on a chair and called for more coffee. 'But the other three are on the loose, though the Avignon police are confident they have them cornered.'

Jean-Pierre invited the two to be seated as a maid arrived with fresh coffee and extra cups.

Unable to still them, Jackie found her eyes straying to Cal's darkly scowling face and was filled with a hopeless emptiness.

'Did you learn anything from the three you have?' asked Jean-Pierre.

Both men shook their heads. 'Two of them are dead, the third we hope to interrogate if we can bring him down from the colossal high he's on.'

As the man spoke, Jackie heard only his initial words and her mind was filled with the lanky, boyish figure of Henri—not as she had last seen him, masked and nervous, but as the rather irritatingly attentive student she had first met.

'Henri,' she whispered hoarsely, addressing no one in particular. 'Is he all right?'

Both policemen gave her slightly puzzled looks, while Jean-Pierre de Perregaux looked positively startled. Only Cal showed no surprise, he was smiling a cold, humourless mockery of a smile.

'One of the two dead men is named Henri Sabine,' replied the second policeman guardedly.

'I didn't know his second name,' blurted out Jackie, unable to stem the sickened protests that shrieked in her mind. No matter what his original involvement—Henri had saved them. 'He didn't deserve to die! Perhaps, had you bothered to speak to me last night, you'd have realised that.' She heard Cal's exclamation of disgust as she spoke, and she turned on him, her eyes filled with hatred. 'He saved you!' she spat at him. 'He risked his life to save us both.'

'Would you like to make a statement, Miss Templeton?' asked the policeman nearer her.

Jackie nodded. It was when she described recognising Henri, despite the mask, that she became aware of the avid interest of both policemen.

'He begged me not to tell Monsieur de Perregaux that I'd recognised him,' she explained.

'But surely it was your duty to tell him?' exclaimed Jean-Pierre, frowning.

'Henri frightened me—he was so different. I can't describe his mental state . . . it was as though the slightest incautious word or action on my part would make him snap.'

The policemen exchanged looks, both nodding.

'You have to put yourself in my place,' exclaimed Jackie wearily. 'I was under a terrible mental strain, and Henri was the only person who had offered any hope. You also have to understand that he was right . . . Cal didn't trust me. Deep down, he felt I was part of the plot.'

Cal shrugged as both policemen gazed enquiringly at him.

'OK, I wasn't entirely honest in my statement. Put it down to de Perregaux chivalry, if you must,' he added dismissively, his words bringing somewhat rueful smiles to the faces of both men.

'Your description fits the man Sabine and what we know of him. He was a heroin addict which accounts for much of the mental state you describe. Both he and his companion were dead when the police arrived—from heroin overdoses. We feel the one we're hoping to interrogate is a similar pawn to the other two—a young addict whom they were forced to use when we rounded up most of the gang.'

Jackie straightened and gazed directly at the man she took to be the more senior of the two officers. 'I should like to know if I'm under any suspicion,' she stated quietly.

He shrugged. 'We find nothing that suggests you are in any way implicated, Miss Templeton. But, for obvious reasons, you will be required to remain here.'

'The reasons are not obvious to me,' stated Jackie.

'Until we have all those involved in custody, both you and Monsieur de Perregaux have to be regarded as being at risk—a very minimal risk, as it happens, but one we have to take into account. No one can leave or enter these premises without encountering our surveillance team.'

'Is this completely necessary?' exclaimed Cal impatiently. 'I've a film waiting to be edited . . .'

'It's completely necessary, *monsieur,*' cut in the man quickly. 'We even have guards at the nursing home in which Madame de Perregaux now is.'

Cal took a sharp breath. 'And our parents?'

'Even though they are in the United States, the authorities there have been alerted. Your parents are protected, *monsieur*. Please understand this is only a temporary necessity—any hour now we hope to have the remaining three of your captors in custody.' He glanced from Cal to Jackie. 'We shall return this afternoon to obtain sworn statements from you both.'

Both detectives rose and bowed politely.

'I'll see you out, and our thanks for all you are doing,' murmured Jean-Pierre, rising too.

'Alone at last,' drawled Cal, helping himself to more coffee as the three left.

Jackie looked across at him: the man who for so long had been her sole companion; the centre of her world; her lover. Her gaze dropped as she felt the hot colour rush to her cheeks. Just as circumstance had hurled them together, now it had torn them apart, and the knowledge, far from bringing her the relief it should, left her feeling only edgy and uncertain.

'I suppose you feel I should be racking my brains for suitable words of apology,' he mocked, refilling her cup.

Jackie shrugged, a habit she had acquired from him.

'Don't strain yourself,' she snapped. 'I shan't go to pieces from the lack of an apology from you.'

'I suppose I have no option but to believe your tale,' he murmured.

To her surprise, Jackie felt a smile, albeit a weary one, creep to her lips.

'You really do find it impossible to admit you

were wrong, don't you, Cal? Not that it's of any interest to me—I honestly don't care what you think any more.'

He caught her by the arm as she rose and made to walk past him. 'Sit down, Jackie—we should talk.'

'Let go,' she said quietly, trying to prise her arm free of the lean brown fingers imprisoning it. 'Your days of bullying me at your leisure are over.'

'What the hell do you mean?' he roared, then suddenly gave a soft, disbelieving groan as he released her. 'Jackie, did I really bully you? Hell, even given the state of mind I was in, there could be no excuse for that!' His dark head dropped as he gazed broodingly down at his feet, and Jackie felt herself stiffen against a crazy urge to run her fingers through his hair—a gesture from which she would undoubtedly have gained far more comfort than he ever would, she thought wryly.

'Cal, we've both been through so much . . . and we're both just over-reacting. You might have a particularly foul temper at times, but you're not a bully.'

He glanced up, the suspicion leaving his face as he saw the glimmer of humour on hers.

'Jackie, won't you sit down . . . please?' he asked softly. 'We'll have breakfast together—just like the bad old days . . .'

'OK—as long as I don't have to sit on the floor again,' she murmured, taking her seat and receiving a smile that had the effect of a minor earthquake on her senses. Trying to distract herself from the upheaval churning away inside her, she watched as he buttered two rolls, her eyes widening as he heaped preserves on to both before handing her one.

'Cal, you wouldn't dunk that . . . would you?' she asked, wide-eyed.

'Sure would,' he grinned, then dunked. 'Jackie, I did bully you,' he stated, his mouth full.

'Cal, forget it,' she pleaded.

'No! God, there were times when I could have killed you! As when I overheard you whispering with that Henri . . . I couldn't even hear what you were saying.' His face was grim as he looked across at her. 'Have you no idea what it did to me—your not telling me? Hell, Jackie, I even asked you if you had anything to say!' he exclaimed angrily.

Jackie gave a silent groan, remembering only too well his words and her interpretation of them.

'Jackie, what in God's name was I to think when you flatly refused to tell me anything?'

'I wanted to tell you,' she whispered miserably. 'I felt your distrust of me . . . saw it in your eyes,' she added hoarsely, conscious that her words explained little.

'I asked you, damn it!' he shouted, flinging down his napkin in disgust.

'Yes, but you weren't the one facing you,' retorted Jackie. 'You didn't see the expression I saw on your face!'

'Jackie . . . please, don't let's fight any more,' he sighed, his anger dying as quickly as it had flared. 'It's strange . . . how circumstances can turn complete strangers into . . .' He hesitated, as though searching for words. 'I don't know what they did to us, but last night, when I'd finished with the police, I found myself automatically seeking you out. Almost as though I needed you—I don't mean sexually—I just needed your physical presence.' He shifted uneasily in his seat.

'I know what you mean,' said Jackie quietly. 'When you're not around, I find myself looking over my shoulder—expecting you to be there.'

'Thank God you're experiencing it, too,' he exclaimed, with a grin of pure relief. 'Perhaps it's a fairly common psychological reaction to what we've been through together.'

'I'm sure it is,' agreed Jackie, finding little comfort in his relieved words—something warned her it would be a long time before she would get used to his not being around. And soon he would no longer feature in her life at all.

'Will you do your teaching diploma when you return to England?'

She nodded, stunned by the terrible bleakness filling her at the thought of her return.

'But what if you're pregnant, Jackie?' he asked, his tone expressionless.

Her eyes met his and she felt suddenly completely alone.

'That's something I should know within the next couple of days,' she stated flatly. It was hardly a lie—except that, by now, she should already have known. 'So let's not waste time leaping to conclusions before it's absolutely necessary.'

'It might be more than a couple of days,' he stated in a curiously detached tone. 'I believe traumas such as you've just experienced can affect a woman's cycle.'

CHAPTER SEVEN

'IF YOU'VE caught them, I can see no need to keep me cooped up here,' exclaimed Cal impatiently. 'My work's been disrupted long enough as it is. Look, I've an apartment nearby from which I usually work when I'm in Paris. If I agree to stay there . . .'

'*Monsieur*, please, just give us time to tie up loose ends,' asked the officer. 'A day at the most, though it could well be merely hours.'

'He'll stay here as long as necessary,' stated Jean-Pierre firmly, giving his scowling brother a withering look. 'In fact, I'd prefer it if he and Miss Templeton kept a low profile till the trial in progress is over—probably the day after tomorrow at the latest.'

Jackie flashed him a sympathetic look as his patently disgruntled brother flung his large frame on a deceptively fragile-looking period sofa and glowered uncooperatively. Two days in the company of both brothers had left her in heartfelt agreement with their mother's sentiments—Jean-Pierre's temperament was positively angelic when compared to that of his volatile younger brother.

'A couple of days ago you were glad to be alive,' she rounded on Cal as Jean-Pierre and the policeman left. 'Now you're acting the prima donna just because your movements are restricted.'

'And I suppose you think that once the cameras stop rolling, a film's finished,' he scowled.

'Isn't it?' murmured Jackie, her eyes flashing anger. 'Silly me. I thought all they did was post it off to my local cinema. Cal, had no one ever told you what a pompous, patronising prig you can be at times?'

'No one—except you, my darling Jackie.'

She gritted her teeth as he spoke. He had an infuriating habit of using endearments to insult. Yet he rarely used them as they were intended—except in the extremes of passion. She gave an involuntary shiver at the thought. Memories of their shared passion were creeping into her mind with increasing frequency and, despite their altered circumstances, the need for him lived on in her, unsettling her with its growing strength when by now it should be weakening away to nothing.

'What are you thinking, Jackie?' he asked, throwing her with the sudden softness of his tone.

'I think I've insulted you enough for today,' she retorted, trying to inject lightness into her words and failing miserably.

'Don't lie.' He sat up and faced her. 'You and I are too closely attuned to be able to get away with lying to one another.' His words were husky, but it was what she saw in his face—in the eyes that swept in blatant caress over her body—that weakened her control over the need dammed up inside her.

He rose and approached her. 'You see . . . you know what I'm thinking—just as I knew what you were,' he whispered, his hands weightless on her shoulders as they drew her towards him.

'Why did you bother asking, then?' she exclaimed in agitation.

'To see if you'd admit the truth.'

'Cal, please . . . what's the point?'

'The point is that you and I have our separate lives to live. But first we have to lay the ghost of what lies between us.'

'And this isn't the way to do it,' she protested, resisting an overwhelming need to fling her arms around him, to drown in the familiar excitement of his body against hers.

'Perhaps it is,' he whispered huskily. 'Perhaps if we answer the need that still lives in us, but answer it this time in our freedom, we can free ourselves from the past.'

'One for the road, so to speak,' retorted Jackie, an inexplicable hurt welling up in her. 'Or, perhaps, a hair of the dog . . .'

'Stop it!' he rasped, enfolding her in his arms. 'Don't Jackie. Why sound so bitter?' His cheek nuzzled against her hair. 'Perhaps we were expecting too much too soon. Expecting our lives to return to normal with the regaining of our freedom.'

Her arms slid around him as she relaxed against him. For the first time since their escape, she felt almost a whole person—the first time, since their escape, that he had held her in his arms. As the realisation hit her, she pushed violently away from him.

'Whatever we expected, this certainly isn't going to help!' she protested.

'So, what do you suggest?' he demanded truculently. 'We both know cold showers don't work.' He sighed, then dragged his fingers through his hair, giving her a ruefully apologetic smile as he did so. 'One of these days—and it'll be soon, I hope—I'll be cringing with embarrassment at the mere memory of the way I'm behaving now.'

'Oh, Cal, you idiot,' she murmured with gentle understanding, reaching up a hand to stroke his cheek as she spoke.

All it took was that one incautious gesture and they were back in each other's arms, lips clinging and searching against lips, arms enfolding and exploring the familiar contours of bodies that tensed with the ignition of passion.

'One of the most exciting things about you is that you've never been able to hide the fact that you want me every bit as much as I want you,' he breathed hoarsely against her parted lips, his mouth restless and demanding as his arms moulded her body to the hot message of desire in his.

In the furthest recesses of her mind was a small spark of reason, trying to tell her this terrible need was one that had to be brought under control now, before it was too late. But it was her body that blotted out that spark of reason, offering promises to be fulfilled later—but not now. Now there was only the familiar sweet madness possessing her, a madness mirrored in the lean, virile body imparting its sensuous messages of promise to hers.

'How I've missed you,' she breathed huskily, her fingers luxuriating in the silken thickness of his hair. 'Oh, Cal, how I've missed you,' she choked as his mouth repossessed hers in bruising hunger.

It was the sound of voices in the hall that brought a groaned oath from him. And it was the leisurely approach of footsteps that wrenched them reluctantly apart.

'I can't believe I'm saying this,' growled Cal, his words distorted by his ragged breathing. 'But there are times when I find myself almost missing the solitude we shared.' Bringing a ghost of a smile to the stark pallor of Jackie's face with his theatrical eye-rolling expression of discontentment, he took her by the hand and sat her down on one of the elegant sofas. Still with her hand in his, he sat down beside her, his expression far short of welcoming as he watched his brother enter.

Jean-Pierre took a seat opposite them, his eyes reflecting nothing as they flickered over the clasped hands before rising to those of his brother.

Feeling oddly disturbed by that non-committal glance, Jackie drew her hand from Cal's, finding no resistance as she did so.

'Perhaps I should have consulted you first, but you've hardly been at your most co-operative for the past couple of days.' Jean-Pierre's tone was terse as he addressed his brother. 'I've arranged a Press conference for you here—today.'

Cal gave a shrug of indifference.

'I suggest the two of you decide what you're going to tell them.'

Jackie gave a puzzled frown. 'The truth, surely. After all, the police seem to have rounded up all those concerned.' Jean-Pierre's body tensed noticeably. He shook his head. 'The Press have no inkling of what has happened. I've consulted with government officials concerned, and also the police, and both feel it preferable that the truth be concealed, if possible.'

'I was under the impression they believed in freedom of the Press in France,' stated Jackie, disturbed by his suggestion.

'We do,' replied Jean-Pierre. 'No one is suggesting the papers suppress anything—merely that they not be given a story that has so far escaped them anyway.'

'That's splitting hairs,' protested Jackie, glancing towards Cal for a reaction and finding none. 'And anyway, the story is bound to come out when these people are eventually brought to trial.'

'They won't be charged with kidnapping. There's enough evidence to put them away for several life-times each—on charges of murder, drug racketeering, extortion . . . the list is endless.'

'What about the drug addicts you said they'd been forced to use?' asked Jackie. 'The ones roped in to guard us . . . they weren't involved in all those other things.'

'The only one left alive has been declared mentally unfit to be charged with anything . . . the police have also gathered from his rambling that he was well aware that young Henri Sabine planned freeing you, and actively supported him.' He gave a weary sigh. 'Jackie, I'm one of the most passionate upholders of freedom of the Press you are ever likely to meet.' His eyes held a plea. 'But I'm also a realist who, by profession, is well acquainted with the workings of the criminal mind. Don't you see that publicity would very likely create a spate of carbon-copy kidnaps? I don't want my family, nor the families of my colleagues, put in jeopardy.'

'But there was nothing you—nor anyone in your position—could have done to comply with the kidnappers' demands,' argued Jackie.

'Yet it didn't stop them trying. Just as it wouldn't stop others if they were desperate enough,' pointed out Jean-Pierre quietly.

'No,' sighed Jackie, her expression contrite. 'Jean-Pierre, I'm sorry if I sounded as though I was being awkward—I didn't mean to.' She hesitated, her cheeks flushed with guilt. 'I should have seen the possible repercussions without your having to point them out. Of course I'll do anything you wish to protect your family, and those of your colleagues.'

'Thank you,' he murmured, the patent relief in his gentle smile only increasing her feelings of guilt. 'So . . . what do the pair of you intend saying to the Press?'

'That we've thought things over and have decided not to get married,' replied Jackie with alacrity, turning to Cal in surprise as he let out an exclamation of protest.

'No,' he countermanded. 'We tell them we're engaged, and after a decent interval a statement can be issued to the effect that you've changed your mind.'

'For heaven's sake!' exclaimed Jackie in disbelief. 'What's the point in going through a rigmarole like that?'

'There's every point——' interjected Cal impatiently, only to be silenced by his brother.

'Jackie, not living in this country, you can hardly be expected to know the celebrity status Cal has here—a fact which it wouldn't pay you to ignore . . .'

'What my brother is trying to put delicately,' interrupted Cal harshly, 'is that you'll be branded as a girl I picked up on location and took off with for a few days' fling.'

'What's to stop them looking at it like that once the engagement's called off?' she asked, perplexed by his sudden anger.

'By then, not only will interest have died down a bit, but you'll be safely back in England, where Cal's name means little to the Press,' explained Jean-Pierre gently. 'He's right to want to protect your reputation.'

Cal sighed as he turned to her. 'You've no idea what it could be like if we agreed to your statement,' he murmured, shaking his head. 'There would be no subtlety to the questioning to which they'd subject you. The type of French journalist who takes such salacious interest in the lives of celebrities is crude and to the point in the questions he asks.'

Jackie looked from one to the other with an expression of weary exasperation. She was more than a little touched by their determination to protect her, but she felt their method of doing so verged on the extreme.

Aware that she was weakening, Jean-Pierre smiled appealingly. 'You'll have forgotten all about it by the time we call it off. By which time something else will have caught their interest, and anyway, Cal will no doubt give a heartbreakingly convincing portrayal of the jilted suitor.'

'Not too convincing,' chuckled Jackie ruefully as she capitulated. 'If he's that much of a celebrity, his fans might feel like lynching me.'

'I'll temper my performance accordingly,' promised Cal with a lazy grin as he leaned over and picked up the phone that buzzed beside him. 'Claudia! Yes, I . . . no . . .' He gave an indulgent chuckle as he tried unsuccessfully to get words in. *'Chérie,* of course I've tried to contact you. I've been ringing all over the place, but no one seemed to know where you were.' He pulled a small face and briefly held the receiver away from his ear as an irate feminine voice berated him. 'I take it you've missed me,' he chuckled infuriatingly, and received another verbal blast in response.

As she sat beside him, listening to the softly laughing seduction in his voice, Jackie found herself experiencing several most disturbing feelings—the most prominent of which was a stomach-churning blast of straightforward jealousy. Vainly trying to push from her mind the vivid picture of Claudia Goddard's breath-taking, dark-haired beauty, Jackie's eyes fell to the line of the lean, dark-clad legs that stretched out to cross at the ankles as Cal leaned further back against the sofa. Then her eyes moved to the gleaming wood floor beneath his feet, remaining fixed there as she willed herself to find comfort in the knowledge that soon the madness of the past days would be behind her. Soon her mind and her senses would recover, and her irrational and grossly distorted reactions to Cal would be a thing of the past.

'I know I have a lot to explain . . . *chérie,* of course there's an explanation.'

There was nothing insulting in his use of endearments to Claudia Goddard, thought Jackie, and was stunned by the primitive savagery of her reaction.

'No—you'll have to come here . . . Claudia, just come here, then I'll explain.' There was an edge of impatience to his voice. Then he replaced the receiver and glanced across at his brother.

'I only gave the true story to those of your colleagues I knew you'd want informed,' apologised Jean-Pierre.

'I realise that,' replied Cal with a small shrug. 'But Claudia will have to be told—I owe her that. Don't worry, she can be trusted completely.'

'As you wish,' murmured Jean-Pierre. 'But you'll . . .' He broke off as the phone rang again.

'For you,' announced Cal, handing him the receiver then turning to Jackie. 'It's probably best if I do all the talking to the Press; I'm used to them. They'll want a few photographs, but the whole thing shouldn't take too long.' He turned to his brother, who was just replacing the receiver. 'What time are they due? Jean-Pierre? For God's sake, what's wrong?' he exclaimed anxiously, peering up into his brother's face.

'Nothing's wrong!'

Jackie gave a gasp of surprise as the normally restrained Jean-Pierre let out a whoop of delight.

'That was the nursing home—this time Marie's really in labour. I'm going to be a papa!'

Cal leapt to his feet, and Jackie watched in amazement as both brothers began an abandoned dance of delight around the furniture.

'I'm going to be a papa!' chortled Jean-Pierre, releasing his brother and yanking Jackie to her feet, twirling her dizzyingly around.

'That's wonderful, but shouldn't you be going . . .'

'My God, what am I doing prancing round here?' he exclaimed, returning the laughing Jackie to her seat and gazing around in bewilderment.

'I'll drive you to the nursing home,' chuckled Cal. 'You're in no state.'

'No—I'll pull myself together,' said Jean-Pierre, making a concentrated effort to do just that. 'Besides, you have the Press arriving any minute now . . . I'll ring the moment I have any news.'

'Are you sure he's capable of driving?' chuckled Jackie, a hint of seriousness beneath her laughter as she watched Jean-Pierre dash from the room. 'I don't think I've ever seen anyone as excited as he is.'

'He'll be OK,' murmured Cal. 'Actually, he's not usually as subdued as he's been since you've met him. He misses Marie desperately and he's also frantic in case something goes wrong—not that he'd ever admit it.'

'He must love her very much,' mused Jackie, her words wistful.

Cal pulled a small face as he rose and gazed down at her. 'The pair of them are quite nauseatingly besotted with one another—one might have thought, after six years of marriage, that the novelty would have worn off by now.'

'What a horrid thing to say!' exclaimed Jackie in disgust.

'Jackie, by now you should have learned when not to take me seriously,' he sighed, his eyes oddly guarded as they met hers. 'I only hope I'm blessed with a marriage like theirs when the time comes . . .'

'Excuse me, *monsieur,* but the journalists have arrived.' They both turned as the maid spoke from the doorway. 'They've been shown into the library.'

'Thanks, Colette,' acknowledged Cal, taking Jackie by the hand and raising her to her feet. 'And now's the time for us to do a Jean-Pierre and Marie,' he grinned. 'Think you can manage it?'

'I wish I'd never agreed to this,' groaned Jackie, feeling suddenly inordinately nervous. 'Cal . . . do we really have to?'

'We really have to,' he laughed, slipping an arm round her and gazing down at her with unconcealed amusement. 'Just leave all the talking to me . . . and for heaven's sake, stop looking so terrified.' He stooped, grinning as he teasingly rubbed his nose against hers. 'I'd give you a little peck of encouragement,' he murmured huskily, his open mouth brushing softly against hers, 'if I didn't know from experience precisely what any sort of kiss encourages us into.'

'Cal, please . . . could we get this over and done

with?' she pleaded, her words breathless because his mouth still hovered so near hers and because there was no will in her to move from it.

'What—the kiss or the Press?' He let out a yell of indignation as she butted his chin with her head.

'Serves you right,' she observed unkindly. 'Let's go.'

'Hell, my tongue's practically severed,' he complained, his arm still around her as they made their way through the hall. 'Jackie, I can hardly face this lot with blood spouting out of my mouth like this!'

'Like what?' she demanded, as they came to a sudden halt.

'Like this!' he exclaimed indignantly, sticking his tongue out at her.

She struggled in vain against the laughter bubbling up inside her. 'Cal, there's nothing wrong with your tongue,' she managed weakly.

Glaring disbelievingly at her, he licked the back of his hand and peered at it.

'You see,' she giggled. 'Not even one tiny speck of blood.'

But the smile froze from her face as he flung open the door before them. It was a large room, as beautifully proportioned as all the others she had seen in this magnificent house, each of its four walls lined from floor to ceiling with books—not that Jackie had even recognised them as books. Her eyes were mesmerised by what appeared to be a sea of faces confronting them, and her ears were recoiling from the sudden babble of unintelligible questions greeting their appearance.

She winced as Cal's voice seemed to boom from beside her eardrum and demand order. Then she listened with a mixture of horror and admiration as he parried several, what could well have turned out awkward, questions with a string of lies that left her quite breathless.

As she listened to Cal waxing romantically eloquent, she became aware of the unmistakable scepticism on the faces of several of the note-taking men before them. And she could hardly blame them, she thought, stifling a disbelieving groan of her own. Cal might be a great director, but he was an out-and-out ham when it came to acting.

When it eventually came to the photographic session, she could quite cheerfully have throttled him—he was virtually directing it! She felt her face was about to crack from the fixed smile on it as he positioned her beside one of the long, silk-draped windows, then shifted her a little to the left before cupping her face in his hands.

'Put your arms round my waist,' he instructed softly, tilting her head and gazing down into her upturned face. Despite the flashbulbs twinkling around them, she felt herself responding to the languor creeping into his eyes as they held hers, and even as she acknowledged that response she was hating herself for experiencing it, and hating him for the hold he had over her which she felt he was now exploiting.

'But you wait till you see them, a couple of those shots might well be fantastic,' he exclaimed, plainly bewildered by her angry outburst the instant they were safely alone.

'I don't give a damn how they turn out!' she retorted furiously. 'I'm not one of your mincing starlets whose only objective in life is to make sure she's photographed from the correct angle!' She was perfectly aware that she was over-reacting, and badly, but the words kept pouring out of her. 'And I'm not like you—with the ability to spout a pack of lies like that without even batting an eyelid. And another thing,' she raged, unable to stop, 'no one in his right mind would have believed you! My God, did you actually listen to the drivel you were coming out with? You even managed to sound positively romantic—you, of all people!'

'Surprising though you obviously find it, I'm quite capable of being romantic—when I choose,' he hurled back at her. 'The trouble with you is you're so bloody self-righteous at times, you'd kill any such tendency stone-dead even in a dedicated romantic! My only regret is that I didn't throw you to them and let them shred you to pieces!'

Jackie leapt to her feet and stormed towards the door. 'I'm sure you would have, if it hadn't been for your brother,' she accused unkindly, even though her conscience instantly recoiled from the injustice of that accusation.

'You'll be able to leave the moment you get the go-ahead from the police,' he yelled after her. 'And that won't be a moment too soon as far as I'm concerned!'

She was close to tears as she made her way to her room. His retaliatory words were reverberating in her mind, wounding her with a savagery she felt her own unforgivable outburst could never have inflicted on him. And her outburst had been entirely unforgivable—the whole wretched scene with the Press had been engineered solely for her protection, she reminded herself miserably. Everything that was decent in her cried out for her to return and apologise to him, but something far stronger in her held her back. She asked herself if that something was pride, as she flung her clothes from her and ran a bath. She shook her head angrily, her action bringing hot tears spilling down her cheeks. Her pride had never before prevented her from admitting it when she was in the wrong.

Whatever its name, it held her back now, making it impossible for her to do what she knew she should. And it was exhaustion from the conflict raging on inside her that later eventually pushed her into the thought-free oblivion of sleep.

'Jackie, are you all right? May I come in?'

Her eyes flew open at the sound of that familiar voice and the impatient rapping on the door. She struggled upright, feeling sluggish and disorientated, realising she had fallen asleep on top of the bed, still wrapped in her damp bathrobe.

'Yes—I'm OK,' she called, switching on the bedside-lamp, then leaping off the bed. 'Cal, I honestly didn't mean what I said,' she began, reaching the door just as he was elbowing it open. 'I don't know how I could have said . . .' Her words petered to a stop as she caught sight of the tray in his hands. On it was an ice-bucket, from which protruded a champagne-bottle, and two slender tulip glasses. She watched in bewilderment as he placed the tray on the bedside-table.

'You're forgiven—as long as you disregard the equally revolting things I said to you,' he grinned, removing the bottle and testing it for coldness. 'Let's hope this doesn't curl up and die from the shock of the sudden reduction in temperature—I didn't feel there was time enough to cool it as it deserves,' he muttered with obvious concern as he stripped away the foil.

Jackie found herself trying to look suitably sympathetic, while privately wondering how one chilled champagne correctly—plainly not by dunking it in an ice-bucket, judging by Cal's very Gallic concern.

Dragging her still-groggy mind away from her newly discovered ignorance, she found herself puzzling over not only his presence, but his noticeable change in humour. 'Cal . . .'

'Glasses!' he ordered, easing off the cork.

Jackie picked up the glasses, her expression openly puzzled as she held them out while he poured.

'What's the English expression?' he queried, taking one of the glasses and causing the fine crystal to give a richly melodious ring as he touched rims with hers. 'Wetting the baby's head?'

'Cal!' she gasped, clasping her hand to her mouth in consternation and delight. 'The baby—what did she have?'

'A great brute of a female—judging by its weight—over four kilos, if my gibbering brother's to be believed,' he grinned happily and drained his glass.

'That's . . it's just wonderful!' exclaimed Jackie and immediately drained hers. 'I bet Jean-Pierre's over the moon.'

'Further then that—he's practically delirious,' he chuckled, refilling their glasses, then seating himself on her bed. 'He's convinced he's the first man in history ever to have become a father.' He patted the bed beside him.

Jackie was laughing as she sat down next to him. 'What are they calling her?'

'Natalie—among a string of other names,' he

murmured, raising his glass once more. 'To Natalie.'

'To Natalie,' echoed Jackie. 'That's a lovely name.'

They drained their glasses in unison, then had another for good measure.

'How does it feel to be an uncle?' asked Jackie, having to steady the hand holding the glass he was yet again refilling.

'Positively exhausting,' he murmured proudly. 'Care to drink to it?'

'Love to,' Jackie responded happily, a deliciously carefree light-headedness wafting through her. 'To beautiful Uncle Cal.'

'To beautiful Uncle Cal,' he repeated, his eyes twinkling over the rim of his glass at her.

'What I meant to say was that you'll make a beautiful uncle,' she explained with earnest concentration, having quenched her thirst once more. She held her glass out automatically for a refill.

'Do you think that's wise?' he chuckled.

'What—thinking you'd make a beautiful uncle?' she asked, practically shoving her glass under his nose.

'No—having more to drink. Jackie, there's no point mincing words, you're tiddly—what have you eaten today?'

'I can't remember—but I feel quite thirsty.' She blinked in bewilderment as he gave a soft laugh and took the glass from her.

'Champagne isn't a thirst-quencher,' he chided, placing both glasses back on the tray. 'Especially not on an empty stomach, as I suspect yours is. Come on, we'll get some food into you.'

'I don't want food,' she protested, then surprised them both by flinging her arms round his neck. 'Oh, Cal, I'm so pleased we're friends again. I hate it when we fight—but this time it was definitely all my fault. Have you really forgiven me—or are you just being nice because you're happy about the baby?'

'Jackie, you're throttling me,' he croaked.

'Cal, I'm sorry!' she exclaimed, loosening her frantic hold, her hands and eyes anxious as both minutely examined him for signs of damage.

'I don't know about sorry,' he sighed, slipping his arms lightly around her. 'But tipsy, if not downright drunk, you must certainly are.'

'I'll not react to that slanderous remark,' she informed him. 'After what I said to you, you're allowed at least five—no, make that three—hateful remarks before we're even.'

'Are you sure it doesn't warrant five?' he murmured, straight-faced.

'Let's call it four,' she conceded.

'Done. Jackie?'

'Yes?'

'I've forgotten which of the terrible things it was you said that warrants all this contrition.'

'The one about throwing me to the Press had Jean-Pierre not stopped you . . . anyway, that's the only terrible thing I said,' she added indignantly.

'What about accusing me of spouting drivel?' he asked innocently. 'And implying I wasn't romantic?'

'Well, no one in her right mind would describe you as roman . . .' She clapped her hand over her mouth to silence her lapse, then looked on in bewilderment as his head dropped to her shoulder and his body went limp with convulsed laughter.

'Cal?' she murmured, frowning. 'Cal!' she shrieked, yanking him up by the hair. 'What's so excruciatingly funny?' she demanded irritably, then took an audible gasp of breath as she found his face so very close to hers.

It was a beautiful face. The most perfect, excitingly masculine face she had ever seen. The hand that reached up to explore and caress that perfection was frustratingly steered from its course.

'Jackie, our first priority must be to get you sobered up,' he told her firmly.

'Why?' she demanded, no longer bothering to claim she was in any way sober.

'Because, whether you realise it or not, you're too bewitchingly seductive in your present state, and I'm not sure how long I can go on resisting you.'

'Why should you want to resist me?' she whispered, her fingers curling their way into his hair.

'Because I don't want to take unfair advantage of you,' he protested huskily.

'What would be unfair about it? I want you just as much with a couple of glasses of champagne in me as I do without,' she pointed out softly, her head suddenly completely clear.

'But the champagne's bound to make a difference,' he argued half-heartedly, as her fingers moved to the buttons of his shirt and began undoing them.

'You're not putting up a very good argument,' she admonished, yanking his shirt from inside his trousers and sliding it off his shoulders. 'After all, you were the one who suggested this as a way to get us out of one another's systems,' she added, as he accommodatingly made it possible for her to remove his shirt completely.

'I know, but you didn't show much enthusiasm for the idea,' he muttered, eyeing her with alarm as she suddenly slid off the bed, landing somewhat heavily at his feet, where she began removing his shoes and socks. 'Jackie, what the hell do you think you're doing?' he demanded warily.

'I m undressing you,' she murmured, admiring her handiwork and deciding his feet were as perfect as the rest of him.

'You fell off the bed—which proves you're drunk,' he accused, hastily withdrawing the foot she had begun caressing.

'I didn't fall off the bed. I had to get down here to remove your shoes,' she informed him patiently, then rose and gave him a push that sent him sprawling across the bed.

'Jackie ' he protested, as her fingers deftly unbuckled his belt. 'You wouldn't dare,' he chuckled softly, propping himself on his elbows, his eyes challenging as her fingers faltered.

'Oh, wouldn't I?' she retorted, allowing herself no time for second thoughts as she unzipped his trousers and began yanking them off him. 'You could at least help!' she exclaimed crossly, tugging harder as the weight of his body impeded her efforts.

'Jackie, for God's sake!' he choked, laughter exploding from him as she suddenly went flying backwards and landed in a heap on the floor.

'Didn't need your help, did I?' she gloated, triumphantly waving his trousers aloft.

'Are you capable of getting up?' he teased through his laughter.

'I'm not drunk,' she retorted, leaping agilely to

her feet, then gazing down at him from where she stood between his long, tanned legs. 'I admit it went to my head at first,' she murmured, leaning forward and trailing her fingers lightly across the muscled flatness of his stomach. Excitement and triumph shivered through her as she heard his sharp intake of breath. 'All that exercise involved in getting you undressed seems to have sobered me completely,' she murmured, her fingers now rippling through the dark hairs of his chest.

'I'm only playing hard to get because I'm still convinced it's alcohol making you behave like this.'

'Are you calling me a liar?' she asked softly, revelling in the sudden shiver of excitement hurtling through him as her hands trespassed further.

'Yes,' he groaned, his legs vice-like as they suddenly imprisoned hers.

'And is this your idea of playing hard to get?' she asked even more softly, as he sat up and slipped the robe from her body.

'Jackie, promise me this has nothing to do with the champagne,' he begged huskily, burying his face against the fullness of her breasts.

A soft moan of longing escaped her as she felt the familiar sweetness of his probing mouth on her flesh, and her arms crossed possessively around him, holding him to her as her trembling hands explored the firm muscled contours of his back.

'You're my champagne, Cal,' she whispered as he drew her down on the bed on top of him. 'Only you can affect me like this.'

He rolled her to her back, their legs still clinging as though loath to relinquish even the smallest area of contact, and there was the sultry darkness of desire in the eyes that gazed down into hers.

'Jackie, tell me you've been going out of your mind just as I have,' he pleaded hoarsely, his cupping, exploring hands sending hot shivers of longing coursing through her as they checked the secrets that fate had made familiar to only him. 'Tell me that all you've wanted is this,' he demanded urgently, the turbulent need of his body goading hers beyond reason with the reckless sensuality of its promise.

'I wanted to fight it—but I can't,' she moaned, her hands impatient against the soft cotton of his shorts. 'Oh, Cal, will there ever be a time when my arms won't feel empty without you?'

'Never,' he groaned, his promise as reckless as the passion that swamped them, that drove them beyond the already impossible delights they had known before. And it was as though each had been stripped of almost every inhibition, and only the magic of the perfect chemistry between them held the primitive force of their passion from tipping them over the edge to insanity.

There came a moment when he seemed to sense the devastating power unleashed in him, when he tried to rein it in, begging her not to feel fear. And it was the totality of her response that dispelled his uncertainty, goading him with an abandon that allowed him unrestrained freedom, till release was a devastating explosion that left them both panting and sobbing in one another's arms.

It was in that moment of aftermath, when he gazed down at her tear-stained face and made no attempt to deny the glitter of tears in his own eyes, that Jackie knew that the confusion of feelings tormenting her had no other name but love.

CHAPTER EIGHT

'CAL.' His name whispered on to Jackie's lips as she woke and turned to seek him, just as they both had turned, seeking to find one another, time after time in the stillness of the night. But this time she found only the silken coolness of sheets, gently ruffled where his body had lain.

'Cal?' she murmured once more, then lay back against the pillows, a hesitant smile creeping over her lips as she began to stretch, then felt the tingling protest of a body still tender from the ravages of passion.

'Cal,' she sighed, his name singing within her as she rolled over and buried her face in the pillow that had held his head, hugging it to her as the elusive, almost spicy masculine smell of him wafted over her.

Her mind—her power to reason—had been temporarily blocked, no doubt by the trauma of her recent experience. It had been so obvious that she loved him . . . all those glaring symptoms—yet no diagnosis until that sudden moment of clarity last night! The only problem was, it was a diagnosis Cal had yet to make. Suddenly she sat bolt upright, startled by the unexpected swiftness of the fear sweeping through her. Of course he loved her. His symptoms were identical to hers, she pleaded with that fear, it was just that Cal was taking longer to face their cause then she had.

'Jackie, tell me that you've been going out of your mind just as I have.'

She had—because she loved him. Then she was shaking her head, her hands pressing futilely against her ears as she tried to blot out other words now in her mind.

'. . . you and I have our separate lives to live. But first we have to lay the ghost of what lies between us.'

She heard so many of his words; insistent words that refused her frantic attempts to silence them.

'One of these days—soon, I hope—I'll be cringing with embarrassment at the memory of the way I'm behaving now.'

Her face pale and tense, she went into the bathroom and took a shower, silently cursing the fate that had topped its callousness with the cruellest blow of all. On top of everything that had happened to her, she was now desperately in love with a man who, had circumstances been normal, she would never even have known. And all he wanted was a return to normality, she informed herself brutally, slipping on a cool cotton dress and belting it so tightly that she was forced to loosen it. All right—so they shared the same symptoms—but the headache heralding the onset of a mild cold could be every bit as severe as the one predicting a lethal brain tumour.

There was a new awareness in her eyes as she made her way from her room to the terrace. Though Cal's references to his privileged background always contained a strong element of mockery, there was a now an overwhelming consciousness in her of the gulf between their worlds—his, a fairy-tale of wealth and beauty—

hers . . . Her steps faltered momentarily with a painfully vivid picture of the cosy, though by no means opulent, home she and Nadine had shared, and loneliness spread within her, engulfing her with its all-pervading bleakness.

'Jackie? Is anything wrong?'

'Jean-Pierre! I didn't expect to see you. Congratulations,' she stammered as the tall Frenchman rose politely from the breakfast-table, his expression anxious as he saw her exhausted pallor. 'It's such wonderful news,' she exclaimed, her face brightening. For a second she hesitated, then reached up and kissed his cheeks.

'I still can't believe it!' he sighed, giving her a hug that dispelled her fears that her greeting might have over-stepped the bounds of their acquaintanceship. 'She's such a beautiful baby,' he enthused, drawing out a chair for her. 'I've always thought babies rather ugly—but you should see Natalie—of course, she looks just like her mother,' he added by way of a slightly sheepish apology, and busied himself by pouring Jackie some coffee. 'I embarrass myself, the way I keep going on . . . but I just can't stop talking about her!'

'And why should you stop?' chuckled Jackie sympathetically, realising just how fond she had become of this quiet, often almost shy man. 'Tell me all about her—has she any hair?'

'Lots—and black. Marie's very fair, so perhaps she'll change—though Marie hopes not.'

No, thought Jackie, Marie would obviously want her baby to look just like the husband she adored . . . who adored her.

'Jackie, it's so good to have you to talk to,' grinned Jean-Pierre, passing her a basket of croissants. 'I think my brother's beginning to doubt my sanity.'

'Where is Cal?' murmured Jackie, grateful and a little surprised to her how casual the words sounded.

'He's had to go off to sort out his love-life,' chuckled Jean-Pierre, oblivious of Jackie's sharp intake of breath as he turned and picked up several newspapers from the chair beside him, then began making space for them on the table. 'Seems the beautiful Claudia wasn't too pleased to see these.' He pushed the papers towards her.

His words ringing like a death knell in her, Jackie tried to concentrate. Cal had certainly known what he was talking about when he had said the pictures would be good—even she could appreciate that they were extraordinary. But it was what they seemed to be shouting to the world that disturbed her profoundly. Yesterday, when he had cupped her upturned face in his hands and gazed down at her, there had been no thought of love in her mind. But it was there before her in print; there in her eyes, in the parted expectancy of the lips that seemed to be raised to his—there for anyone to see who chose to look.

'They're brilliant photographs,' murmured Jean-Pierre appreciatively.

Jackie watched him guardedly from beneath lowered lashes. He obviously had not seen it . . . was she only seeing it through the eyes of a suddenly over-active imagination?

'I thought he was going to warn Claudia,' she stated, amazed to hear herself sounding no more than a mildly interested bystander.

Jean-Pierre pulled an unsympathetic face. 'So did I—but apparently he didn't get round to it—so he's had to go haring off to pacify her now.'

Jackie looked at him in alarm.

'No—it's OK,' he assured her hastily. 'He checked first with the police and they've given the all clear. In fact, you're free to return to England whenever you please. Of course, they'll need to be able to contact you, not that they're envisaging that being necessary.' He paused, then surprised her by reaching over and taking one of her hands. 'Jackie, I hope I don't have to tell you how welcome you are to stay here for as long as you like.' He frowned as she made to protest, an impatient frown that suddenly accentuated his strong resemblance to his brother. 'Your holiday was ruined, to put it mildly, through no fault of your own.'

Jackie pulled a small face. 'You're being too generous. It was through my ludicrous, unthinking gullibility.'

'Through no fault of yours,' repeated Jean-Pierre stubbornly. 'And Marie's longing to meet you, she's been asking me all about you. Jackie, I know you and she would get on . . .'

'Jean-Pierre, it's very sweet of you to offer,' she butted in gently, touched by the obvious sincerity of his words. 'I'd love to meet Marie—and the baby. Perhaps, when I've got myself sorted out at home, I'll be able to . . . but there's so much I have to sort out . . . my entire life, in a way.'

Jean-Pierre's warmly sympathetic probing quickly elicited the sadness that had taken her to Biarritz.

'My dear, I had no idea,' he muttered, aghast. 'How will you keep yourself while you train as a teacher?'

'If it comes to it, I can always sell the house and buy a flat. Actually, the solicitor mentioned some insurance Nadine had taken out.' She hesitated. 'In fact, there are so many things the solicitor wanted to discuss with me . . . I kept making excuses to put off seeing him . . . I just couldn't bear the thought of it . . . neatly tidying up . . .'

'No, I can understand that,' he interrupted quietly, deliberately disrupting her painful train of thought.

'But now the time has come for me to face reality,' she said firmly.

'You say you might have to sell the house, but would you wish to?'

'I honestly don't know,' she sighed. 'One of the things I have to find out is if I could continue living there . . . with all the memories.'

He reached over and patted her hand.

'May I tell Marie that once you have everything sorted out you will return to us in Paris? A holiday to start you off in your new life.' His smile both questioned and encouraged.

She gave a tremulous laugh. 'Jean-Pierre de Perregaux, you are an exceptional man. And I'm very glad to know, from what I've heard from Cal, that you have a wife who is very much aware of the very special man she has for a husband.'

'Oh, yes,' he grinned. 'I'm always telling Marie just how special I am.'

It was the gentle teasing in his words, and the small bow accompanying them, that reminded Jackie with such painful sharpness of his brother, a reminder so disruptive to her peace of mind that her hand was shaking as she raised her cup to her lips.

'What time are you going to the nursing home?' she asked, in as normal a voice as she could muster.

He glanced at his watch. 'In about half an hour. I'd invite you along, but I'm afraid it's fathers only for the first few days—they're very strict. But Cal should be back before I leave.'

Cal had not returned by the time his brother left. In fact, it was late in the afternoon when he eventually made an appearance. In the intervening hours, Jackie's mind had acted out virtually every permutation of what their meeting might entail.

Her mental state had teetered through all the stages between wild elation—imagining his tall figure striding towards her, then his taking her in his arms to tell her of the love he had just discovered—and abject misery, as she heard the relief in his voice as he told her he was now free of the tiresome spell fate had cast on him.

As it was, he did none of the things she had so meticulously anticipated. And even her exhaustive permutations had not run to his arriving with this tall, breathtakingly beautiful woman clinging to his arm.

Claudia Goddard was dressed in a simple, biscuit-coloured dress. Its neutral shade should have done nothing for the smooth olive of her tanned skin—it managed to do just about everything. Just as the deceptively plain cut of her dress gave discreet accentuation to every curve of her perfectly proportioned body.

'Jackie, meet Claudia,' announced Cal, looking at neither woman as he flung himself at full stretch on to a sofa and immediately closed his eyes. 'I'm whacked.'

'Now, there's breeding for you,' murmured the film actress drolly, then smiled as she stretched out her hand to Jackie. 'It's good to meet you, Jackie.'

Jackie managed a routine pleasantry as she returned the warm handshake, before her facial muscles gave out on her completely. And her mouth was like sandpaper, she realised with an element of panic, her eyes flying to Cal's inert form in the vain hope of support as Claudia took a seat. As far as she could see, he was asleep.

'He's been like that nearly all day,' chuckled Claudia, noticing Jackie's glance. 'The trouble with these blue-blooded aristos, they have no stamina,' she added conspiratorially. 'And few manners either, come to think of it. Is there any chance of a drink in this museum, or is the place dry?'

Jackie felt an involuntary grin come to her lips, instantly warming to the beautiful Frenchwoman who was a household name even in the English-speaking world.

'Jackie, be a love and ask Colette to fix us some drinks,' muttered Cal drowsily.

'Colette being one of an army of slaves, I take it,' murmured Claudia, grinning as Jackie went to find the maid.

It was the expression on the actress's face when the uniformed maid eventually arrived with a tray that eased much of the tension from her and even brought her spontaneous laughter. She also found herself gaining a completely irrational comfort from the realisation that the beautiful actress had obviously never visited Cal's home before.

'So, Jackie, have you recovered from your terrible ordeal yet?' asked Claudia, kicking off her shoes and tucking her long, shapely legs beneath her. 'It must have been ghastly,' she added sympathetically.

'It's beginning to seem rather like a bad dream,' replied Jackie. 'I'm sure, once I'm home, I'll hardly be able to believe it really happened.' The stab of pain brought about by the mere mention of leaving was sharpened by the sudden memory that Cal also had a flat in Paris. Had he and Claudia spent the day there?

'Jackie?'

'Sorry,' she exclaimed distractedly, appalled by her thoughts and the effect they were having on her. 'I didn't catch what you said.'

There was a hint of concern in Claudia's warm brown eyes as they flickered over Jackie's pale, tense face.

'I asked if you knew when you'd be returning to England,' she repeated gently.

Of their own accord, Jackie's eyes moved to the sprawled figure of the man she loved.

'Tomorrow,' she announced firmly, her chin lifting a fraction. 'Yes, I'm going home tomorrow.

'What do you mean, tomorrow?' demanded Cal, suddenly sitting up.

'Jean-Pierre told me the police have agreed,' replied Jackie, torn by the conflicting interpretations her mind was churning out in response to his patently negative reaction to her announcement.

'Yes—they've agreed that we can leave the house,' he retorted, rising and pouring himself a drink.

'Only a de Perregaux would describe this place as a house,' interjected Claudia in a loud whisper, and gave Jackie a broad wink.

'But surely not to leave the country,' continued Cal, flashing Claudia a withering look.

'And of course, your fiancé,' chuckled Claudia, completely unwithered. It was when he slammed his glass down on the table with a force that might easily have shattered it that her amusement turned to surprise.

'The police have no objection to my leaving, as long as they can contact me if necessary,' stated Jackie, her heart thudding. Her eyes rose to his as, in silence, he picked up his glass once more and raised it to his lips. The eyes that met hers over the rim were like chips of ice. 'They don't seem to think there will be any necessity to contact me,' she continued, unnerved by the silence and using the words merely to fill it.

'So . . . you're leaving tomorrow, then?'

'Yes.' Jackie's eyes dropped to the glass in her own hands, wondering if the chill in the growing silence was as obvious to Claudia as it was to her. Of course it was, the girl would need to be comatose to escape it. Her fingers tightened convulsively round the glass. When Jean-Pierre had referred to Cal sorting out his love-live, it was of Claudia he spoke . . . Claudia was Cal's love-life Her eyes rose, bitter antagonism in them as they met the ice in his. 'Yes, I'm leaving tomorrow.'

There was no shred of sensitivity in him, she told herself angrily. She could, at a pinch, excuse his ignorance of her own feelings. But not those of Claudia. He obviously cared enough about the girl to need to explain his fictitious engagement to her—but, having done that, he seemed oblivious to her possible reaction to a scene which, at the very least, Claudia must find puzzling.

Emotionally drained, and unable to guarantee that she wouldn't end up making a complete spectacle of herself, Jackie rose and placed her glass on the table beside her. Forcing a smile to her lips, she turned to the now pensive Claudia.

'It was lovely meeting you, but I'm afraid I should start sorting my things for packing.'

'But I'll see you this evening . . . won't I?' asked the girl, her eyes questioning as they turned to Cal.

For several seconds he returned her look blankly, then gestured impatiently with himself. He turned to Jackie. 'I've invited some people round this evening—some friends and people I work with.'

'If you don't mind, I'll have an early night,' said Jackie. She had to get out of here! Her mind was playing grossly disturbing tricks on her, superimposing the soft sensuousness of passion on the cold aloofness of his face.

'I suggest you have a rest now. It would look odd if my fiancée weren't present this evening.'

Jackie's lips tightened angrily, and she was conscious of the close scrutiny of Claudia's eyes.

'If they're your friends, surely you'll be telling them the truth!' she exclaimed.

'As my brother so rightly pointed out, the fewer who know, the better. Only a handful of people present tonight will know . . . to the rest, I'm a newly betrothed man.'

'It should be interesting, seeing you with your style cramped,' murmured Claudia, with more than a touch of sarcasm.

'This isn't a joke!' he rounded on her.

'No,' sighed Claudia, looking genuinely contrite. 'It isn't. I'm sorry . . . it's just so difficult to grasp all that's happened.' She turned to Jackie. 'And his brother's right—the risk of others copying it is too terrible to contemplate.'

Jackie nodded in weary agreement. 'I'll be there tonight, Cal.' Desperate to do something to alleviate the unbearable strain in the atmosphere, she gave Claudia the ghost of a smile. 'I could do with a few acting lessons, though,' she murmured wryly.

She had taken the fact that she had no idea what she should wear and whipped it out of all proportion, forcing it to dominate her every thought till it eventually had the desired effect and stifled the desolation of what was truly on her mind.

When she had packed for Biarritz, it had been a last-minute decision to include something formal, and even then she had only done so because the sight of the dress hanging in her wardrobe had brought Nadine's words of only three months before creeping back into her mind.

'Who cares if you've no occasion to wear it right now—a time will come, and it won't date. It's in love with you, *chérie*. See how it hugs itself to you!'

There had been undeniable pleasure in Jackie's laughter as she had seen her own reflection; the creaminess of her skin accentuated by the rich dark green, the slim curves of her body taking on a new voluptuousness beneath the caressing cling of the soft fabric.

There had been no opportunity to wear the dress—neither in England nor in Biarritz. And now it lay on the bed, vivid and almost exotic beside the other two dresses she had tentatively considered. It was probably far too formal.

If only she had thought to ask Claudia, she berated herself, then shrugged; whichever she chose, she would end up either over or underdressed.

She looked at her watch, and frowned. She had no idea what time it would start. Then she froze, as she heard a light tap on her door, before hastily rising to answer it.

'May I come in?' asked Cal, his tone distant and formal.

She opened the door wider to admit him, her heart sinking as her eyes drank in the dark-suited elegance of the aloof stranger who was also her lover.

'They'll be here soon,' he stated, frowning to see her still robed. 'I suppose I should have told you what time they were expected.'

'I suppose I should have asked,' she countered stiltedly, wondering why he felt it necessary to enter her room—he could have said what he had at the door.

'Jackie . . .' he began, then dried up completely.

'What?' she demanded coldly, gaining a perverse satisfaction from seeing him uncharacteristically fumbling for words.

'About last night, I didn't mean . . .'

'Cal!' Her sharp cry of his name silenced his words. Silencing him was the only means she had of protecting herself from the dreadful inevitability of the words she never wanted to hear. To him, last night had been a mistake. He was reunited with Claudia now, and his passion of the night before had become an embarrassment and a regret. She accepted that, but she still could not bring herself to hear the actual words. 'Cal, last night is behind us . . . the past is behind us,' she stated, her voice firm as every dream that had ever been hers turned to dust inside her. 'Neither of us need feel embarrassment . . . you were right, we needed last night to lay the ghost of the past.'

'And now it's laid?' he demanded hoarsely.

'Yes—now it's laid.' She turned from him, unable to trust what her eyes might call out to him. 'And another thing . . . you'll be relieved to hear I'm not pregnant.'

'You're not?'

'I'm not.' She repeated the lie firmly, though the knuckles of her clenching hands were stark white as she spoke.

'That's . . . it's great news.' His expression was dazed as he moved and sat heavily on the edge of the bed. 'I suppose it'll take time before it sinks in.'

'Not too long, I hope,' managed Jackie, having to tear her eyes from the sight of him, from the memory of shared laughter as, only hours before, she had sat at his feet to remove his shoes and socks. 'I have to get dressed,' she added in a strangled voice.

'Jackie . . . what's wrong?' he asked, in a voice as distorted as her own.

'Nothing's wrong!' The words choked in her throat. 'Yes, it is, I don't know what to wear. I've nothing suitable.'

After several seconds' silence, she began to

wonder if he had heard her. Then he rose, glancing down at the three dressess on the bed.

'The green,' he stated abruptly.

'Are you sure it isn't too formal?'

'Put it on and I'll see,' he instructed coldly.

She hesitated, hating her spirit as it deserted her and began to wilt beneath the mockery in the cold smile that crept to his lips.

'You don't really expect me to turn my back while you get into it, do you?' he drawled.

'Yes, I do,' she retorted, loathing him for what he was doing to her and arming herself with that loathing as he slowly turned his back to her.

'You may look now.' She was glad of the glimpse of what she saw in those grey-green eyes before he managed to bring down the shutters of indifference over them. It told her desire still lingered on in him, despite his intention to relegate it to the past.

But not for long, she realised with a shiver of utter hopelessness. And anyway, she was fooling herself. She knew what the dress did for her, and Cal was a man renowned for his appreciation of women. His eyes had shown no more than what she would have found in any other responsive and virile man.

'It's not too formal,' he told her abruptly, glancing down at his watch. 'Two things, though, before we go down.' He put his hand in his jacket pocket and drew out a small leather box. 'Jean-Pierre dug this out—you'd better wear it.' He opened the box and took out a ring.

Jackie knew her eyes were widening in disbelief as they caught sight of the ring's single stone—a huge emerald-cut diamond. 'I can't possibly wear that,' she gasped. 'Whose is it?'

'It's part of the family collection,' he replied, pulling a wry face. 'It's the ring I shall give to the woman I eventually marry.'

Jackie's hands clenched nervously behind her back as she wondered if he had noticed her visible recoil from his words.

'I don't know why you're making such a fuss,' he exclaimed impatiently, noting her reaction and putting his own interpretation on it. 'Jean-Pierre feels that, having announced our engagement, we might as well give the story as much credence as possible, and I agree with him. Give me your hand.'

'You're both overdoing it,' she argued stubbornly, feeling an almost superstitious aversion to the idea of wearing the ring.

'Give me your hand!'

Glaring at him, she held out her hand.

'This finger?' he queried, hovering between the ring and middle finger, and eventually opting for the correct one.

'Yes,' she snapped. 'At least you'll know the correct one when you come to doing the job properly.'

'Alway assuming I ever get round to doing it properly,' he retorted, ramming the ring on her finger.

She gazed down at the huge, sparkling stone, then angrily shoved her hand behind her as it ridiculously crossed her mind that his future wife would need fingers as slim as hers—it was a perfect fit.

'You said two things,' she stated coldly. 'What

was the other?'

'Your hair,' he replied his eyes holding hers in cool challenge. 'You know I don't like it like that.'

Before she realised his intention, his hands were in her hair, removing the comb and scattering the restraining pins around her as his fingers wrought their havoc.

'I don't give a damn what you like!' she retorted furiously.

'Leave it!' he ordered, as she immediately began twisting her hair up once more.

'I'm not one of your servants,' she hissed. 'If I want it up, I'll wear it up.'

He grabbed her by the wrists, dragging her hands away from her hair and sending the slender straps of her dress tumbling off her shoulders as he forced her to lower her hands. His eyes seemed to become transfixed by the sight of those fallen straps, and she heard his sharp intake of breath in the instant in which he released her hands.

'Forgive me,' he muttered hoarsely, taking a dazed step back from her. 'I honestly don't know what came over me. Of course you must wear your hair in whatever way pleases you.' He turned, as he spoke, and went to the door. Then he stopped, his face pale and tense as he half turned before leaving. 'There's a buffet on the terrace—come down when you're ready.'

Jackie felt her hands, her entire body, shaking uncontrollably as she picked up her brush and began dragging it distractedly through her hair.

He might not understand what had come over him. But she did. The bond originally imposed on

them had turned to love for her. For him, it had
been a bond from which he needed to escape.
Only, his body had lagged behind his mind in
realising that—rearing up in a display of purely
physical male dominance before finally stepping in
line with the requirements of his mind.

And now he was free, she told herself numbly,
stooping to pick up the scattered hairpins. She
picked them up, placed them on the dressing-table,
then ran her fingers through the rich thickness of
her hair, leaving it hanging in a carefree cloud that
floated around her shoulders.

'This is the way that pleases me, Cal,' she
whispered sadly, but there was only her own
distraught reflection to hear her words.

'By any standards, Cal is behaving appallingly,'
rasped Jean-Pierre, open fury on his handsome
face as he spoke. 'Nearly everyone here thinks he's
engaged to you—yet he's spent the entire evening
draped over Claudia Goddard!'

'You're exaggerating, Jean-Pierre,' protested
Jackie, forcing a smile to her lips. He wasn't
exaggerating, objected the gaping wound that was
her mind; if anything, he was grossly understating
the facts.

'I can't tolerate it—it's an insult to you . . .'

'Jean-Pierre, it's . . .'

'For heaven's sake, Jackie, stop protecting him!'
His face softened as he saw her pleading look. 'All
right, go and find him and get him to dance with
you,' he sighed, then frowned. 'And what on earth
possessed him to let them start all this dancing? It
was meant to be a quiet buffet supper.'

'It's the score for his new film,' muttered Jackie,

under no illusions now as to whether both brothers had been cursed with the legendary de Perregaux temper—she wondered how long it would be before Jean-Pierre's finally blew . . . and whether Cal would live to see tomorrow.

Her glance moved disconsolately towards the dancing couples. She too would have given anything for there not to have been dancing. Though it had both hurt and surprised her that, having perfunctorily introduced her to several people as his fiancée, Cal had then given his exclusive attention to Claudia. But what had ripped through her, savaging her with the brutality of its hurt, was the way he had taken Claudia in his arms when, having sat and listened critically to the soundtrack for a considerable time, he had decided to dispense with business and give himself up to pleasure.

What she had seen, before she had managed to drag her anguished eyes from the mesmerising sight, now remained indelibly inscribed on her mind. Etched in her mind was the pale lavender of Claudia's dress, starkly outlined against the dark-suited, lean athleticism of his body. She could still see the way the girl's flawless body had melted against his, drawn close by the strong, tanned hands whose fingers had begun tracing their secret, sensuous messages against the smooth bareness of her back.

'This is ridiculous! Where is he now?' exploded Jean-Pierre, his patience finally snapping as he looked in vain for his brother among the swaying couples. 'I've had enough of this—I'm finding him and having it out with him!' There was fury on his face as he leapt to his feet.

'Jean-Pierre, please,' begged Jackie, placing a restraining hand on his arm.

'I'll kill him for this!'

'Please . . . a scene will only make things worse. I'll find him and bring him back . . . tell people we've had a tiff, or something,' she added half-heartedly, wondering how much more of this she could take.

'You know where he is—where they are?' he asked grimly.

Jackie nodded, pain heaping on top of pain within her as her mind replayed the image of Cal's arm, firm as it encircled Claudia and coaxed her out on to the terrace.

'OK—no scenes, I promise. Bring him back here—we'll see what we can salvage from this fiasco.'

Feeling physically sick with apprehension, Jackie took reeling steps towards the one terrace door remaining open. Leaning weakly against the cool wood of the frame, she had to force her protesting body to take the next few steps that would bring her out on to the terrace.

In the silvery darkness, it was only the paleness of Claudia's dress that first stood out, its smooth line broken by the dark bands of the arms encircling her body.

'Cal, I don't think you'll ever know how relieved I am your engagement isn't a real one,' Claudia was murmuring huskily. Then further words were silenced by the lips that descended to possess hers.

Jackie reached out, grabbing a nearby chair for support as she felt her knees buckle under her.

'Cal, Jean-Pierre wants you inside—immediately.' She forced the words from her, expelling them before she lost courage and ran.

'Does he?' he drawled, his dark head rising as Claudia turned in his arms. Despite the darkness, she sensed the glittering coldness in his eyes—eyes that an instant before would have contained the darkness of passion. 'Tell him I'm busy.'

His words brought the beginnings of a death to her. 'No, I shan't,' she stated, disgust spilling into the quietness of her voice. 'For once you'll just have to put aside your own selfish requirements and think of others—the safety of your own family, for instance.'

'For God's sake, Cal, she's right!' exclaimed Claudia, freeing herself from the arms that still held her.

'Yes, I'm right. I'm the one you talked into this situation. I'm the one who was forced even to wear a ring to enhance the pretence. I'm beginning to wonder why you bothered to persuade me into any of it . . .'

'He's too damned persuasive for his own good,' exclaimed Claudia guiltily. 'Cal, I told you this was irresponsible!'

Yet she found him irresistible, noted Jackie, a strange feeling seeping through her, almost as though a switch inside her had been flicked—turning off all emotion.

'My brother's got you well trained,' he drawled unpleasantly, fury in his eyes as he strode towards her. 'Pity he's already married—you fit into the de Perregaux mould to perfection.'

Jackie's eyes flickered over his dishevelled figure in disgust. 'Your mouth's covered in lipstick—I suggest you remove it, only because it bears no resemblance to mine.'

He was selfish and unprincipled—unworthy of the love she had so carelessly given him. The love which was already beginning to die in her, she told herself triumphantly, never stopping to wonder where her surge of strength had come from, or whether it might have anything to do with the strange emotional limbo in which she now hovered.

CHAPTER NINE

'JEAN-PIERRE, I can take a taxi to the airport; you go and visit Marie,' insisted Jackie.

As they sat at a table on the terrace having late morning coffee, a light breeze swept gently along its length, pleasantly cooling the sting of heat from the sun. Jackie's eyes swept appreciatively over her now familiar surroundings, delighting for a moment on the spray that fanned in uniform clouds of diamonds from the sprinklers on the softly rolling lawns before them. She was going to miss this place, the sheer beauty of it, she thought sadly, then started as she felt Jean-Pierre's hand on her arm. She looked across into his smiling face.

'You haven't heard a single word I've been saying,' he chuckled. Then the smile disappeared beneath a scowling frown. 'You weren't thinking about last night . . .'

'No, Jean-Pierre, I definitely wasn't thinking about last night,' she told him firmly. 'And if I were, it would be only with relief. Are you sure no one suspected anything?' she added anxiously. 'I feel so ashamed of myself, losing my temper and stalking off like that . . .'

'Jackie, as it turned out, it was the best thing you could have done. I have to admit it, my irresponsible brother looked every inch the frantically remorseful betrothed as he dashed after you. And Claudia Goddard went up in my estimation by giving a beautifully understated performance of one realising she had been used in order to make you jealous.'

Jackie flashed him a decidedly sceptical look. 'Surely no one would believe Cal would behave as juvenilely as that.'

'I think they'd have believed him capable of anything, given his appalling behaviour . . . I know I almost would.' His face was grim. 'I can't think what got into him . . . it was so completely out of character.' He sighed, shaking his head. 'Did he offer any explanation to you?' His eyes widened in alarm. 'Jackie, I'm taking it for granted he has apologised to you.'

'I'm afraid I didn't give him the opportunity,' said Jackie quietly. 'Jean-Pierre, Cal and I have been through a lot, and it will probably be a long time before we're back to normal.'

He nodded understandingly, relief and a tinge of guilt creeping into his eyes. 'I should have taken that into account last night. God knows, I was so angry it didn't even enter my mind,' he exclaimed. 'You're a very understanding young lady, given the humiliation he subjected you to,' he added gently.

Jackie shrugged uncomfortably. 'I understand, but I haven't it in me to forgive—not that it really matters; my life and Cal's aren't likely to cross again.'

'Are you saying you won't be coming back?' he asked quietly, his eyes scrutinising her.

'No—of course I didn't mean that,' she protested guiltily.

'Good, because Marie would never forgive me if she didn't eventually meet you.' He gave a soft laugh. 'What I was trying to tell you, when you went off into your trance, was that I'd dropped in to see her after I collected your ticket.' His eyes twinkled mischievously as they met hers. 'I have strict instructions to see you safely off. I've a feeling she's timing me—I think I'm supposed to stand and wave your plane out of sight before returning to the nursing home.'

Jackie chuckled. 'I do love the sound of your Marie—I'm really looking forward to the day we actually meet.'

She glanced up as she spoke, everything freezing to a halt in her as Cal strolled out on to the terrace. His eyes were dark and heavy with exhaustion, and he looked as though he might have tumbled from his bed, except that the short black towelling robe he wore, and the still wet hair clinging to his head, indicated he had very recently stepped out of a shower.

'Jackie, I need to speak to you,' he stated quietly as he approached the table and sat down. 'Alone,' he added pointedly to his brother.

'I don't think she wishes to speak to you,' replied Jean-Pierre, his tone glacial.

'I wish to make my apologies,' stated Cal, his tone as expressionless as the eyes now on Jackie.

'There's no need,' blurted out Jackie, horrified to find the cloak of emotionlessness that had cocooned her in its protection ever since last night now slipping from her. 'I accept your apology,' she gabbled. 'There's no need to say any more.'

'Oh, but there is,' he murmured, showing no sign of reaction as the cup he had picked up slipped from his fingers and smashed to pieces at his bare feet.

'Cal, are you all right?' demanded Jean-Pierre, frowning as his brother glanced, almost in surprise, at the pieces by his feet, then leaned down and began picking them up, placing them one by one with concentrated care in the saucer from which he had originally lifted the now smashed cup.

'I'm all right,' he replied, his eyes never once straying from his task. 'All I want is the chance to apologise to Jackie—alone.'

Slowly shaking his head, Jean-Pierre turned to Jackie, his expression anxious and questioning. With every nerve in her body tensing in protest as she did so, she nodded in weak acquiescence.

'I'll be in the library, there's something I need to look up,' he told her, a mixture of relief and apology in his eyes as he rose and left.

Cal showed no sign of even having noticed his brother's departure, his body having taken on an almost robotic rhythm as it dipped then rose as he lifted particle after particle of the broken cup.

In silence, Jackie watched him, the protective cloak now stripped from her completely as her eyes became mesmerised by his movements, lingering on the muscle at the side of his neck that swelled then subsided with the hypnotic rhythm of his movements. Her eyes were practically caressing him, she realised aghast. Then her face tightened, her eyes losing their warmth as her mind drove her back to the night before, to the scene on this very terrace. And her eyes became slits of ice as they searched the lips which had offered the secrets of their passion to lips other than hers.

'Is this your idea of an apology?' she demanded, her tone a cold contrast to the agonised heat within her. 'This resounding silence?'

'I don't want you to go.'

'What's wrong, Cal?' she sneered. 'Didn't Claudia live up to your expectations?' Even as the bitter words leapt from her, she was desperately trying to snatch them back.

'You might have got me out of your system—but you're still in mine.' His eyes rose, dark with hostility as they met hers. 'I want the freedom you've achieved.'

'You've already achieved that freedom!' She didn't even hear the bitterness in her words, she was too busy trying to ward off the kaleidoscope of pictures flitting through her mind: Cal with Claudia in his arms, his hands caressing her body, his lips hungry on hers; Cal with the woman for whom he wished to be free. 'You showed that by your behaviour last night.' She jumped up, terrified she was on the verge of giving her innermost secret away.

'Jackie, I didn't mean to hurt you like this,' he groaned, rising and barring her escape.

'You didn't *hurt* me,' she retorted coldly, desperately hanging on to her control. 'What you did was *humiliate* me. Ironic, isn't it? I was the one coerced into this farce of an engagement—to protect your family. I was the one forced to wear a de Perregaux knuckle-duster to lend credence to the farce.' She tried to stem the words pouring from her, but they wouldn't stop. 'And I was the one who, for the sake of your family, allowed herself to be made a spectacle of by you in front of a roomful of people who were under the impression I loved you! Where were all your noble thoughts of your family's safety when you were so publicly making love to Claudia last night?' Her voice dropped to a scarcely audible whisper. 'When it really gets down to the basics, the only thing that matters to you is getting what you want. Last night you wanted Claudia . . . and to hell with everyone and everything else. I don't want any apologies from you, Cal—don't waste your breath by insulting me further.'

'Jackie . . . please . . . I didn't mean to insult you . . . it's the last thing I'd ever want to do to you,' he whispered hoarsely.

She felt the anger draining from her, sapping her of energy. 'Cal, does, it matter?' she sighed wearily. 'The only thing that should really matter to us it that we're alive. We should forget all this and just be thankful for that,' she added tonelessly, wondering if a day would ever come when she would be able to heed her own advice.

'How can I forget you?' His tone was dazed.

'You already have—in the way you wish to—it just hasn't sunk in yet, that's all,' she replied, turning and walking away from him in the moment she felt herself wanting to beg him to take her in his arms just once more.

She walked away slowly, all the while willing herself not to turn back for one last look at the man with whom she was leaving all the love she possessed.

'It's lovely—bright and airy—and blissfully tranquil.' Ann Watkins nodded in approval as she finished her inspection of the small living-room and sat down, her eyes alert as they turned to the girl who was not only her patient, but also one of her closest friends.

'I haven't bought it—just rented it,' explained Jackie, stretching over to the tray on the small coffee-table before her and pouring out two cups of tea. 'There's an identical one coming up on the market soon, so I've a while to see if this really suits me. I . . .'

'Jackie,' interrupted Ann sharply. 'Aren't you going to ask me the result?'

'It's positive,' replied Jackie calmly, passing her a cup.

'Yes . . .'

'Ann, deep down I think I knew even before I left Paris . . . six weeks later, you can hardly expect me to show any surprise.'

Ann Watkins placed her cup on the table, her gaze purely professional as she examined the soft beauty of the oval face opposite her. There was the darkness of exhaustion beneath the wide-spaced blue eyes, and the pallor she had noticed when Jackie had first returned from France was still there.

The two girls had met almost five years before, when Ann had joined her uncle's practice, replacing the surly old Scottish francophile who had always sworn he had delayed his retirement only because of his unrequited love for Nadine.

At first, the thought of a girl only a few years her senior being Nadine's doctor had troubled Jackie. But her fears had disappeared at almost their first meeting. Both she and Nadine had taken to Ann instantly, and a very close friendship had quickly developed between the three of them.

'Jackie, why didn't you say anything to me about this before I left for that course?' asked Ann unhappily.

'Because I know you—you'd have started flapping and tried to postpone it,' smiled Jackie.

'But the thought of you being alone for almost a month . . . going through all this . . .'

'All what, Ann?' chided Jackie gently. 'I told you before you left that I was putting the house on the market. Those two weeks in it after I came back told me I couldn't live there any more.'

'I meant your pregnancy,' exclaimed Ann sharply, kicking off her shoes and tucking her legs under her. 'Despite what you say about knowing, you must have been on tenterhooks waiting for me to come back so you could take the test . . . Jackie, why didn't you go to Uncle Bob? You know he's not the sort to lecture you or anything.'

'I know that,' protested Jackie. 'Ann, I want this baby, I want it more than you'll ever know. The only reason I took the wretched test, and it only coincided with your return, you'll be irked to know, is because I panicked the other morning . . . I suddenly thought—what if I'm not pregnant, what if it's all in my imagination?'

Ann gave her a look that queried her sanity.

'I'd been feeling ghastly in the mornings,' explained Jackie. 'But that particular one I felt fine—that's why I panicked.' She gave a rueful smile. 'I'm back to starting my days with a mad dash for the loo,' she added, sounding noticeably contented.

It was that innocent contentment that tore through Ann. 'You must love him very much,' she whispered sadly, recoiling from the sudden anguish and tension her words brought to that pale face. 'Jackie, this is someone who loves you who's prying, as well as your doctor. You can't keep it all bottled up inside you. You've got to talk about him . . . it could end up destroying you.'

'You knew I was in love with him when I first came back,' Jackie told her hoarsely. 'Even though I only told you the bare bones of what had happened.'

Ann nodded. 'I also saw how you resented my knowing . . . and the terrible bitterness in your resentment worried me.'

'I couldn't bear the thought of anyone knowing. I'd had to hide it from Cal—from Jean-Pierre—from everyone.' There was an empty bleakness in the eyes that met Ann's. 'The thought of anyone seeing it without my having said anything—even you, Ann—my pride just couldn't take it that you might not have been the only one to see through me.'

'It would take someone who knows you as well as I do,' said Ann gently, hesitating slightly before continuing, 'Am I right in thinking there's another woman in his life?'

'Yes—Claudia Goddard,' replied Jackie bleakly, managing a ghost of smile as she saw her friend's reaction to that famous name. 'Powerful competition, you might say?'

'I suppose that's one way of putting it,' sighed Ann, taking a gulp of tea. 'But you'll have to tell him about the baby.'

'I know . . . but not until after I've had it.'

'Why then?' demanded Ann. 'Why not now?'

Jackie hesitated only briefly before speaking, then told Ann all that had occurred during the time she and Cal had been held in captivity. Though the frankness of her telling opened up wounds that had scarcely even begun to heal, she also found it had a strangely cathartic effect on her, and the pain, when she had finished speaking, wasn't quite as bad as she had feared.

Ann drew her hands across her face, a gesture that indicated uncharacteristic confusion. 'Jackie, the man you've just described . . . by no stretch of the imagination could he be called irresponsible,' she said, frowning deeply.

'He's not . . . I wasn't trying to imply he was.' She had never thought of him as irresponsible—not until he had disillusioned her so callously the night before she had left. But even Jean-Pierre had been shocked by that . . . She dragged her mind away from such thoughts. 'It was the way he kept bringing up the subject of abortion . . . Ann, that's the reason I don't want him knowing about this baby until after it's born!'

'Why—because you think he'd be able to pressurise you into having one?' asked Ann sceptically.

'Of course he wouldn't be able to,' retorted Jackie indignantly. 'It's just that I couldn't bear to hear him suggest it,' she whispered unhappily.

'And you think he would?'

'I've just told you his attitude,' exclaimed Jackie, puzzled by her friend's suddenly almost clinical manner.

'Perhaps you've left something out,' murmured Ann.

Her reply was Jackie's emphatic shaking of her head.

'So—as I see it—he brought up the subject of abortion, and you refused to discuss it.'

'There was no way I wanted to discuss it,'

replied Jackie. 'Who knows, perhaps I was already in love with him then, but I was quite prepared to have his baby . . . I told him that.'

'Only after you had become lovers—when, in fact, you could already have been pregnant.'

'Yes. And he immediately dragged up the subject of abortion again,' exclaimed Jackie bitterly.

'And once again, you wouldn't let him have his say.'

'I didn't have to!' shouted Jackie, starting guiltily as she heard the aggression in her voice. 'Ann, I'm sorry . . .'

Ann waved the apology aside, lost in thought. 'Jackie, did he ever mention this Claudia Goddard—I mean his relationship with her?' she asked suddenly.

'No . . . but I should have known. He was staying at the hotel with her.'

'With her?'

'I don't know. But I'd seen him with her. And he was meeting her the night I intercepted him.'

'So, he obviously wasn't sharing a room with her.'

Jackie shrugged. Ann's questioning was getting her down. What she needed was a bit of friendly sympathy, not this third degree.

'Jackie, has Cal contacted you since you've been back?' asked Ann gently. She realised how Jackie was reacting to her questioning, but her instinct, both as a friend and professionally, urged her to continue.

'Yes!' The word was a cry of pain as Jackie buried her face in her hands, her slight shoulders heaving from the harsh sobs racking her.

'Jackie, love, this is what has to come out of you,' she whispered gently as she went and crouched by her sobbing friend. 'This terrible volcano of hurt bubbling so furiously inside you.' She put her arms round her and rocked her gently.

'I know,' choked Jackie. 'But I've gone over and over it in my mind, trying to free myself from the pressure of it that's building up inside me . . . but it doesn't help . . . it just won't go away!'

'I'm going to to make us a fresh pot of tea.' Ann told her huskily. 'It won't harm you to have a good cry.' She got to her feet, tears in her eyes as she stacked the tray and made her way into the tiny kitchen. No, it wouldn't harm Jackie to have a good cry, she told herself sadly, but the poor girl had probably cried her fill in the past weeks, and it certainly hadn't done her any noticeable good.

When she returned, she was greeted with a wan, slightly sheepish smile.

'If you still feel like having your ear well and truly bent, I suppose I might as well explain what happened in Paris.'

This time the pain that came with the telling was savage, and it was a pain unrelieved by any feeling of catharsis.

'Ann, I keep torturing myself . . . seeing him with Claudia in his arms,' she whispered distraughtly. 'The pictures won't go away.' She rammed her clenched knuckles against her trembling lip. 'I keep seeing him . . . making love to her, just as he once did to me . . . Ann, it's horrible . . . depraved almost . . .'

'It's common-or-garden jealousy,' cut in Ann,

her tone completely matter-of-fact. 'Jackie, how does he contact you—does he write, phone?'

'He phones . . . at least, he used to phone.'

'Why did he stop?'

'He hasn't the number here. I didn't even give it to Jean-Pierre and Marie . . .'

'Because you didn't want them to give it to Cal?' Jackie nodded.

'Don't they find that odd—your not letting them have this number? They're both obviously very fond of you.'

'I lied—I said there wasn't a phone here. But they have Nadine's solicitor's number if they need to contact me . . . and I ring them regularly.'

And Marie, the warm, friendly girl whom she had yet to meet, couldn't wait for her to get the house sold and keep her promise to visit Paris again.

'What did Cal say that upset you so?' asked Ann gently.

'What he's always said!' exclaimed Jackie angrily. 'I'm not out of his system and he wants me out of it! He wants to use me till he no longer wants me!'

'But you say he has Claudia.'

'Don't you understand? It's because of Claudia—for her—that he wants to be rid of me!'

'Jackie, I find it difficult to believe that he'd put it as brutally as that.'

'He doesn't have to,' she retorted wearily. 'Ann, do you think I don't realise how all this must sound to you?' she groaned. 'But, as a doctor, you must know there are psychological repercussions from an ordeal such as Cal and I went through. There was nothing normal about the relationship that was

forced on us . . . nor the way in which it developed.
I was a virgin, for heaven's sake—yet practically
within hours, the centre of my life became making
love with a man who had been a total stranger until
the day of our incarceration! Ann, I've no idea
when I fell in love with him . . . but I needed him
like a drug—just as he needed me.' She dragged her
fingers distractedly through her hair. 'And that's
why I can understand what he wants—as no one
else could. Through no fault of his own, he became
hooked on a drug . . . he wants to kick the habit.'

'Jackie, I know what you're trying to say—but
you're interspersing fact with conjecture.'

'Perhaps I am . . . all I know is that I can't take
any more of it. I can't take hearing his voice . . .
he's rung from Italy, from America. Twice he was
so drunk he was almost unintelligible. I have to be
free to forget him . . . just hearing his voice tears
me apart . . . I have to be free.'

'Drink your tea before it gets cold,' urged Ann,
her face pale with worry.

'I *shall* get over him,' promised Jackie, her voice
firming. She lifted her cup, then drained it. 'I'm
going to be a whole person for our . . . for my
baby. His or her life will be a good one.' She
replaced the cup. 'You know, I never thought of
money when Nadine was alive . . . we never wanted
for anything. But once I got up the courage to face
her solicitor, it was to learn that Nadine had left me
what amounted to a small fortune. Thanks to her,
my baby will want for nothing materially
. . . nor in any other way.'

CHAPTER TEN

JACKIE lay on the sofa, her feet up, her head on a cushion propped against the armrest.

'I meant what I said about having a daily siesta,' Anna had nagged affectionately when she had popped round earlier. 'I want you alert and at your most appreciative tonight for the culinary masterpiece I intend producing.'

At least they would be at Ann's place tonight, thought Jackie gratefully; the past week's hectic socialising was beginning to take its toll—though it was good to see Ann so on top of the world now that Clive, her fiancé, was back from his three-month business trip to America.

Clive had brought an American colleague back with him for a couple of weeks, a friendly, if somewhat hyperactive, young man who thought nothing of driving fifty miles to eat in a restaurant he had heard was worth visiting.

Jackie glanced at her watch; it was far too late in the day for this to be termed a siesta, but she certainly needed it. She had immediately seen through Ann and Clive's protective reasons behind drawing her into this foursome—and she knew she had benefited mentally from it—but, with a stab of guilt, she realised she would be glad to see the back of the easy-going and friendly Ed Simpson . . . if only because she would be guaranteed regular early nights.

So much for her late siesta, she thought, grimacing as she rose to answer the phone now ringing in the hall.

'Miss Templeton? John Hogan here.'

Nadine's solicitor, she thought, her grimace deepening. He was one of the few people she had taken an instant dislike to—even the sound of his voice made her hackles rise.

'Mr Hogan,' she stated flatly. The man was pompous, opinionated, and tended to use fifteen words where five would suffice. 'How are you?' she added, guilt brought about by her uncharitable thoughts prompting the question.

'I'd like to be able to say well—but unfortunately I can't. In fact, I'm more than a little displeased.'

'And why is that?' asked Jackie, conscious of the sarcasm entering her tone. One of the things she particularly disliked about the man was his infuriating tendency to talk down to people—women in particular.

'I feel obliged to inform you that I have a drunken foreigner running amok in my office—my office which should have closed seventeen minutes ago, I might add.'

Jackie felt as though a bomb had just gone off in her head.

'He is behaving frivolously with the female members of my staff, while at the same time threatening me with physical violence if I don't divulge your address to him. Naturally, I haven't done so, I've called the police . . .'

'Mr Hogan, I'll be round as soon as I can . . . in a couple of minutes,' grabbed Jackie, her mind a jumble of incoherency.

'I don't think that's wise—the man is dangerous . . .'

Jackie slammed down the receiver, only her
body functioning as she tore to her bedroom and
flung on a jacket—her mind had ground to a
complete halt.

It was pouring, she discovered as she raced to the
garage, where she flung herself into the car and
managed to hit the side wall as she hurtled out in
reverse.

She also just missed the back of the police car
parked outside the solicitor's office, jerking to a
sudden halt only millimetres behind it as she
belatedly registered its presence.

Panting from her mad dash, she too came to a
sudden halt as she burst into the reception area. Mr
Hogan was nowhere in sight; to her left, in front to
of the reception desk, she recognised the
receptionist and one of the secretaries; both were
grinning broadly. To her right stood a uniformed
policeman; if anything, he was grinning even more
broadly than the two girls, and his amusement was
directed at his colleague, a uniformed policewoman who was sitting on the arm of a huge
leather armchair, gazing down with an expression
of almost maternal concern on her young face at
the dark head nestling comfortably on her lap.

The rest of Cal de Perregaux's body was
sprawled negligently on the chair. There were navy
and white leather trainers on his feet; immaculately
cut, dazzlingly white, cotton trousers skimmed the
outline of those long, sprawling legs. A loose navy
sweatshirt topped the outfit, and he looked,
thought Jackie, with no more than a stab of mild
exasperation, all the world as though he had just

strolled off a yacht.

'I take it you know who he is?' murmured the officer beside her, an unmistakable chuckle in his voice.

'Pascal de Perregaux,' she whispered hoarsely, that blissful momemt when she had felt no more than exasperation gone for ever as the wild chaos of love and hate and despair bubbled and boiled within her.

'Sorry, I didn't catch that,' apologised the policeman.

'Pascal de Perregaux,' repeated Jackie.

'Jackie?' That single word was muffled by the cushion of the policewoman's lap. 'Jackie?' he croaked, raising his head and turning it to where she stood. He struggled to sit upright, bewilderment on his face as he dragged his fingers through his hair. 'Jackie, is it really you?' he whispered in French.

'It's me,' she sighed, puzzled that all she should sound was exasperated, when there was so much emotion churning inside her. 'Cal, what on earth do you think you're doing?'

'God knows,' he groaned, lurching to his feet and taking a few staggered steps before swaying before her.

Grabbing hold of him, Jackie turned pleadingly to the policeman who had stepped over to take some of the sudden weight from her.

'Is he being charged with anything?' she asked hoarsely, suffocatingly aware of Cal's arm now heavy on her shoulders and his head dropping to nestle at the curve of her neck.

'There's little evidence of the mayhem Mr Hogan claimed him to be wreaking here,' muttered the officer uncertainly.

'Mr Hogan exaggerates,' chorused his two employees, with unabashed disloyalty.

'And had he wished to press charges, he wouldn't have left the moment we arrived,' said the policewoman briskly.

Jackie noticed the sergeant's stripes on the uniform as the girl rose and approached her, her eyes twinkling their amusement.

'As long as you don't let him loose on the streets,' she chuckled, 'where we'd more than likely have to run him in for being drunk and disorderly in a public place . . .'

'Oh, I promise,' vowed Jackie earnestly. 'I'll take him home immediately.'

'Have you transport?'

'Yes, my car's right outside,' she confirmed, holding firmly on to Cal and trying to guide him towards the door before the policewoman had second thoughts.

'I think you'll need a hand with him,' chuckled her colleague, trying unsuccessfully to transfer the Frenchman's weight to himself. 'Mind you, now he's found you he doesn't seem particularly keen on letting go,' he grunted, as Cal hung on resolutely to Jackie and resisted all the man's efforts. Their unsteady progress towards the car was further impeded when Cal, oblivious of what was going on around him, suddenly took it upon himself to start removing the comb and pins holding up her hair.

'Cal, for heaven's sake,' she begged, wondering what on earth the two police officers were going to make of this sudden diversion.

'Did you put it up to repel me—or someone

else?' he muttered. 'That's much better,' he announced in satisfaction when her hair eventually tumbled free beneath his clumsy ministrations. 'Don't you agree that's much better?' he demanded of his mesmerised escort.

'Oh, definitely,' agreed the male officer, while his female counterpart gave Jackie what could only be termed a look of sisterly understanding.

'I'd say you'd got your hands more than full with this one,' she murmured with a sympathetic grin. 'But, if looks are anything to go on, I'd say he'd be more than worth the bother!'

It was only after they had managed to get him into the car that the thought of luggage occurred to Jackie, by which time Cal appeared to be fast asleep.

She rolled down the window. 'Did you happen to notice if he had any luggage with him?'

Both officers shook their heads.

'He should have had something, he's just come from France . . .'

'Los Angeles,' interrupted her passenger, with total clarity. 'And my bags are probably in Rome by now.'

'So now you know!' chuckled the policewoman.

With a sigh of exasperation, Jackie thanked the two officers and drove off. 'Why is your luggage in Rome?' she demanded, not holding out much hope of a reply.

'Because I was on my way there. It's just that they happened to announce a flight for London after I'd checked in my luggage—so I switched flights . . .'

'Cal, do you mean to tell me you've come here from Los Angeles in this state?' she exclaimed,

having to slam on the brakes hard as she belatedly
became aware of red traffic lights in front of them.

'If by that you mean drunk—no. That came
later—when I realised what I was doing. Believe it
or not, I don't make a habit of getting myself into a
state like this.'

'You could have fooled me,' she retorted
angrily, pulling away from the lights.

'I've only been drunk about half a dozen times in
my entire thirty-two years,' he informed her
indignantly, managing to sound almost sober as he
did so. 'Mind you, this is the third time in the past
five weeks.'

And the other two times, in those five weeks, he
had taken it on himself to telephone her, she told
herself angrily as she brought the car to a halt
before the ivy-clad block of flats which in its
entirety was probably only about half the size of
the de Perregaux mansion in Paris, she reminded
herself with a confusion of conflicting emotions.

'It seems getting drunk is becoming quite a habit
with you,' she observed tartly, wondering how on
earth she was going to get him out of the car and
into the flat. Her mind refused even to consider
what her problems would be once she got him
there.

'Jackie, I know I am monumentally drunk at this
precise moment,' he announced piously, as he
practically fell out of the car. 'But it's a state I
don't intend getting into again—it achieves
nothing, and I honestly can't say I find it even
remotely enjoyable.'

'Why do you get into it, then?' asked Jackie,
disconcerted to find laughter bubbling in her at the
sight of him gingerly supporting himself against

the bonnet of the car.

'Stop cross-examining me,' he complained, then smiled beatifically. 'Are you sure you're strong enough to carry me wherever it is you're taking me?'

'I've no intention of even attempting to carry you anywhere,' she retorted sharply, only to find a treacherous part of her instantly relenting. 'But you're welcome to a shoulder—as long as you don't break it.'

Her offer was a mistake, she realised it the instant his arm encircled her shoulder and started up a suffocating jumble of emotions within her. It was almost like being back in his arms—it *was* being back in his arms—as the familiar spicy smell of him, despite the unmistakable smell of drink also emanating from him, seemed to waft its way into her soul.

She managed to distract herself from what was happening to her, finding herself giving thanks that she wasn't the sort to dwell overmuch on the opinion of her neighbours as she received glacial nods from the middle-aged couple forced to make way as, with both arms round Cal's waist, she heaved him through the main door of the building.

But there were no outside elements to distract her as she watched him flop on the sofa in her tiny living-room and close his eyes.

'Sorry, Jackie,' he mumbled, kicking off his shoes and stretching full out. 'But on top of the booze, I also haven't had much in the way of sleep for the past few days.' With that, he fell fast asleep.

His clothes were soaked, thought Jackie in consternation. She looked at her watch and groaned. Ed would be picking her up in less than an hour! Then her eyes dropped to the sleeping man whose mere presence was creating such a rage of emotion within her. Damp black locks spilled untidily on to his forehead, and the long lashes of his closed eyes spread against his cheeks like soft, silken fans. The shadow of beard already beginning to darken his face lent it an unkempt, slightly rakish appearance. And, as she stood gazing at him, she could feel the fierce strength of the love she bore him welling up in her till there was no part of her free of it, till it swelled within her and flowed over, spilling down her cheeks in the hot release of tears.

She turned, stumbling in her frantic haste to escape, the silent tears turning to hopeless sobs as she realised she could never find escape.

Though she had calmed considerably by the time she had showered and changed, it was a fatalistic calm that accepted that not even time would have the power to free her of Cal. Even without his child to remind her, he would live on in her, and the knowledge lodged like a block of ice in her heart.

She made up a bed in the spare room and, fifteen minutes before Ed was due, she braced herself to go into the living-room and waken Cal.

He came to with scowling reluctance.

'I've made up a bed for you. And there are fresh towels for you in the bathroom, you can take a shower, or a bath—whichever you prefer.' The moment she had made the suggestion, she had nightmare visions of his falling and damaging himself. 'Perhaps it would be better if you just went to bed.'

He struggled upright. 'Have you some milk?' he

muttered. 'I could drink about a litre of it,' he added with a groan.

'I'll get you some,' she told him gently. 'Your room's the one on the left down the corridor. You get into bed—I'd better do something about getting your clothes washed and dried, or you'll have nothing to wear in the morning.'

'Just like the bad old days,' he remarked softly, his eyes not meeting hers as he got to his feet.

Just like the bad old days, Jackie's thoughts echoed sadly, before she managed to collect herself and went to get the milk. She returned less than a couple of minutes later, to find him not in the spare room, but stretched out beneath the quilt in her own bed—his clothes in an untidy heap beside it.

'Wrong room,' she sighed, placing the two-pint carton down on the bedside-table. 'But not to worry—here's your milk.'

He sat up, took the glass proffered, and drained it.

'More?'

He nodded. She refilled the glass and returned it to him.

'You're all dressed up,' he accused, his eyes suddenly focusing on her.

'Yes. I'm going out.'

'Where?'

'To have dinner with some friends. There's plenty more milk in the fridge should you need it,' she added.

'These friends—who are they?' he demanded, his eyes narrowing as he lay back against the bedhead.

Jackie turned away from the scrutiny of his eyes, nervously picking up her brush and running it through her hair.

'It isn't really any of your business, Cal,' she replied tonelessly. 'I'd better get your washing on before I leave.' Even as she uttered the words, the sheer lunacy of the casual intimacy suddenly enmeshing them struck her. He in her bed, cross-examining her as to her plans; she about to pick up his clothes, which she would then set about laundering . . . the whole thing was mad!

Despite these thoughts, she still stooped to retrieve his clothes.

'I notice you haven't put your hair up to deter him—whoever he is,' he observed coolly.

'I've no intention of listening to your drunken rambling over my hair,' she snapped. 'I wear it how I please.'

'Except that Nadine and I know differently.'

They both froze as the doorbell pealed.

'Jackie, I think you ought to put it up,' he stated truculently.

'As I've told you before, I don't give a damn what you think!' she hissed, then marched from the room. She closed the door firmly behind her. If there had been a key in it—she would have been tempted to lock it.

At two o'clock in the morning she accepted the fact that she was not going to get any sleep. Desperate for something to distract her from the thoughts tormenting her, she went to the kitchen, took Cal's clothes from the dryer and began ironing them. And even that was a mistake, she thought bitterly, recoiling as her hands showed every inclination to caress the garments that had adorned that achingly familiar body.

And Ann would have forty fits if she could see her now, she realised guiltily. Though the thorough check-up her friend had given her had shown her in excellent health, she knew it was her mental state that troubled the ever-watchful Ann—and tonight she had immediately spotted something was wrong —not that there had been any opportunity to tell Ann of Cal's sudden appearance.

But mooching around dwelling on her problems in the middle of the night wasn't going to do her baby any good, she told herself firmly, and her baby was the most important thing in her life. With this thought solidly in her mind, she folded the ironing, made herself a hot drink from her depleted milk supply, and went back to bed.

She drifted into sleep with a speed that would have relieved, if not surprised her, had she been aware of it. But it seemed that no sooner had she had found its blissful relief than unfamiliar noises began dragging her out of it. The daylight straggling into the room, together with a disgruntled examination of her watch, told her otherwise. It was half-past ten!

She sat up and swung her legs over the side of the bed. It was as her sleep-disorientated eyes took in the unfamiliar outlines of the spare room that realisation hit her. Cal!

Following immediately on the heels of realisation, and crowding it from her mind, came the nausea—that debilitating, churning queasiness that always threatened eruption and which, on random mornings, would gratuitously fulfil its threat.

She held her position on the edge of the bed, not daring to move so much as a muscle as she prayed that this would be one of those mornings when fate would show a modicum of kindness.

As though in answer to her prayers, her mind
then presented her with a vivid picture of the
magnificent chocolate gateau Ann had proudly
served up the night before. Then her only prayer
was that she would make it to the bathroom on
time—this time her prayer was answered.

It was several agonised minutes before she was
able to drag her racked body to the sink and bathe
her face in the refreshing coldness of water. And
she was still splashing gratefully when she felt her
hair drawn back from her face to be replaced by
the softness of a towel against her cheek.

Then an arm was on her shoulder, drawing her
upright.

There was a numbed stillness in her body,
belying the shrieking chaos laying siege to her mind
and whipping up fear within her of what her eyes
might now see. And in the suffocating silence that
surrounded her as that towel dabbed gently against
her wet face, she kept her eyes tightly closed. But
through everything she felt his presence, sensed it
with every nerve of her tensed body, like an
invasion of her soul.

'Do you feel up to brushing your teeth? I'm
afraid I've already used your toothbrush . . .'

'Yes,' she croaked, silencing that impersonal
voice.

She was forced to open her eyes when the brush
was placed in her hand. But her eyes went no
further than the ribbon of paste on it, bringing
memories of another time—another, faraway
place—when their positions had been reversed.

She leaned over and began cleaning her teeth,
scrubbing and brushing now, just as he had what

now seemed a lifetime ago.

'You're not going to try telling me it was something you ate,' he stated in a voice totally devoid of any expression.

'No—it was nothing I ate,' she replied wearily, dropping the brush and pushing her way past him. 'Excuse me, I have to lie down for a while.'

There were going to be no scenes, she vowed, trying to control the panic rising in her as habit guided her to her own room. No scenes, no hysterics, she promised herself, then gave a small sob of confusion as he realised which room she was in and turned and walked smack into Cal's considerable bulk.

'Get into the bed,' he ordered gently. Then picked her up and placed her on it when she hesitated. 'Get under the cover.' She drew the quilt over her. 'Jackie . . .'

'No!' she shrieked. 'Don't you dare!' The anger suddenly flaring in her was a desperate, protective anger, and it gave her the strength to look at his face for the first time. What she saw was pale exhaustion, and a chilling grimness. 'Don't you dare even say the words,' she repeated hoarsely, watching as his gaze dropped from hers to his feet.

He said nothing as he rammed his clenched hands into the pockets of his trousers. And his gaze never once returned to hers as he walked slowly towards the window to stand with his back to the room.

'What is it that I'm not to say?' he asked eventually, in that same frighteningly empty voice.

'I shan't have an abortion—never!' she cried, her hands spreading protectively across her stomach. 'I don't care what you think—I love this baby—I want it. And not you nor anyone in the entire world can stop me having it!' Her eyes pleaded with his motionless figure. 'I know I blew what little money I had on that trip to Biarritz—I'd no idea Nadine would leave me so much money . . .'

'Jackie, for God's sake . . . stop this!' he groaned, the last vestiges of colour draining from his face as he swung round to face her. 'What's the money got to do with . . .'

'Money is important now!' She gave a choked sob. 'It's important because with it our baby will never lack for material things. There was never any question of his lacking love, but now I have money, too.' She turned, burying her face in the pillow as he took a couple of angry strides towards the bed. 'Just go away!' she sobbed, furiously trying to shrug off the hands that tried to lift her.

'No! I've no intention of going away!' he roared, ripping the pillow away from her. 'And for once in your life, you are going to damn well listen! Whatever gave you the idea I'd want you to have an abortion?'

'It was all you ever spoke about!' she screamed at him, her hands trying to drag back the pillow he now held clutched to him as he half sat, half sprawled across the bed.

'God Almighty!' he groaned angrily. 'It was a subject you never gave me a chance to speak about!'

'No, because I knew what you were going to say!' she raged. 'That's why I had to lie to you in Paris. That's why I wasn't going to tell you until after it was born.'

'Oh, you were actually going to deign to tell me eventually . . .'

'Of course I was,' she exclaimed angrily, giving

up her fight to regain the pillow and turning away from him in disgust.

'Oh, no, you don't,' he rasped, yanking her round to face him once more. 'I want you to see my face—to be able to see yours—when we have this out. And have this out we're going to . . .'

'You being twice my size being a guarantee that you'll get your own way,' she spat at him.

'If it comes to it—yes!' he yelled, then gave a soft groan of disbelief as he released her arm. 'Jackie . . . please, why are we behaving like this?'

'You tell me—you're the one . . .'

'No—*you* tell *me!* You're the one who claims to be able to read my mind! *You* tell *me* what my feelings are about your being pregnant!'

'You want me to have an abortion,' she muttered, suddenly not nearly so sure of what she was saying as his eyes blazed down on her with a fire that seemed to go beyond anger.

'And if I were to tell you that my one fear—what haunted me—was that if you became pregnant you would contemplate an abortion?'

'But I told you I would willingly have your child—I meant it then and I mean it now,' she accused hoarsely, her mind refusing to accept his words.

'Jackie, you told me that while we were caught up in the sort of circumstances few are ever subjected to,' he pointed out, a softness in his voice. 'Paradoxically, the madness of our passion was what helped keep us sane . . . but there were times when we would have sworn black was white, so strong was our need . . . how could I be certain you would always mean what you said then?' He reached out and placed a hand on her stomach, his touch tentative as first, then sure.

Jackie looked down at the lean, strong hand, a terrible confusion creeping into her as its touch seemed to contain the love and protection her own hands aways did. Then her gaze rose to his, falling immediately as she saw the tears in his eyes.

'Cal . . .'

'No, before we say anything, there's something I have to tell you,' he said quietly, his voice so firm that she could almost believe she had imagined the tears in his eyes. 'When I was twenty-three, I fell in love. She was warm and beautiful and generous . . . she was also twelve years my senior. I mention that because, though it was immaterial to me, it was what lay at the root of what happened.'

The stark sadness in his voice told her she had not imagined the tears, and her heart knew she must be a very special woman—this woman he had loved all those years ago.

'It was because of the age difference that she wouldn't even discuss the question of marriage —though marriage was what I wanted more than anything. There was also the fact that she and the husband from whom she was divorced had never been able to have children—the fault having been diagnosed as hers.'

Jackie's eyes remained trained on the hand that had never moved from her stomach, but her heart was pitying the woman who would never have the joy of bearing his child.

'Jackie, you once asked me about my pre-occupation with contraception . . . Nina and I never had the need of it.'

She felt him shift, though his hand remained on her stomach, and through it she could feel the terrible tension in his body.

'Against all the odds—she became pregnant,' he whispered hoarsely. 'And because of her irrational attitude to our age difference, she felt she had placed us both in a trap . . . she didn't tell me. Instead, she had an abortion.'

'But surely you couldn't have held that against her?' whispered Jackie sadly. 'She only did it because she loved you—it must have been the most painful decision of her life!'

'And one that took her from me for ever . . . she died under the anaesthetic.'

'Oh, no!' choked Jackie, her hand covering in comfort his on her stomach.

'So, you see, Jackie, had you ever let me have my say, the last thing I would have suggested was an abortion . . . my attitude is purely subjective and irrational, I know . . .'

'But so understandable,' choked Jackie. 'Oh, Cal . . . if only I'd known. I can see how you loved her . . . what she meant to you . . . I can understand the tears in your eyes . . .'

'Jackie, I . . .'

'Don't feel ashamed,' she whispered. 'Nobody should feel ashamed of loving that deeply.'

He gave her an oddly enigmatic look, then moved away to sit on the edge of the bed, his back to her.

'Cal, I realise how painful it must have been for you telling me that,' she whispered, all the love in her pouring helplessly towards him.

'Jackie, why is it you're so completely off target with what's going on inside me?' he sighed. 'Yes, Nina was my first love, and yes, there will always be pain in my memories of her. But that old cliché about time healing is true.' Suddenly his broad shoulders tensed visibly. 'Jackie, you haven't even asked me why I'm here.'

'I don't have to,' she retorted numbly, dread and hopelessness filling her at his mere mention of the subject.

'Here we go again!' he groaned in anger, dragging his fingers impatiently through his hair. 'Because you already know why I'm here? Just as you knew I was going to demand that you have an abortion, and just as you knew what it was that could bring tears to my eyes!'

Even as she recoiled from the harshness of his tone, she found his words reminding her of the relatively gentle cross-examination Ann had subjected her to.

He turned, shifting his body slightly in order to face her, though his eyes remained hidden behind lowered lids. 'Jackie, it's taken me a long time to sort myself out from the mental havoc created by the ordeal we experienced. My trouble was that I was too clever by half—realising there were bound to be mental repercussions, I felt obliged to rationalise . . . to explain out of existence almost, every feeling I had in connection with what had happened . . . every feeling connected with you.' He gave a grim, humourless laugh. 'If my judgement hadn't been so completely distorted, my preoccupation right from the first—my morbid fear, in fact—of your even contemplating abortion, should have alerted me.'

'Alerted you to what?' she asked tonelessly, something in his voice sending alarm bells jangling off inside her.

'To the fact that, after all those years, I was losing my heart once again.'

'Don't!' she pleaded, as pictures of him with

Claudia in his arms took possession of her mind.

'Does it disturb you that much—the thought of my loving you?' he whispered, his eyes rising to hers in the very moment the savage hurt festering inside her spilled free.

'The thought of your loving *me*?' she choked. 'Aren't you forgetting the truth? What I've seen with my own eyes? How can you speak of love when you've let me watch you chase and woo and virtually make love to another woman right before my eyes? You held her in your arms, you . . .'

'Jackie, don't!' he cried, flinging himself across the bed and trying to take her in his arms.

'Get away from me! You've no idea how I hate you!' she sobbed, pushing him away. 'How could you do that to me? How could you?'

'Do you think I didn't ask myself that question time and time again?' he groaned, forcing her hands aside and pulling her into his arms, burying his face in her hair as she clung, sobbing, to him.

'You could at least have told me you and Claudia were lovers, instead . . .'

'Claudia and I were never lovers . . .'

'I don't believe you!'

'You're damn well going to believe me!' he retorted angrily, grasping her fiercely by the arms and forcing her back from him. 'I admit I was attracted to her while we were making the film, but I've learned it never pays to mix business with pleasure. I suppose there was an unspoken understanding between us that things might develop later . . .'

'They developed, all right,' cried Jackie wildly, uncaring of how she was sounding. 'You were making a meal of her . . .'

'I was behaving despicably! I behaved worse than

the rawest of adolescents! I was using her feelings for me to try to make you jealous,' he groaned.

'Cal, why couldn't you have just told me you loved me?' she asked weakly, strange new emotions—ones she couldn't yet put a name to—hesitantly taking root in her.

'Because I was still busily rationalising everything I felt for you . . . I couldn't bring myself to recognise it as love. Besides, I'd just been given my marching orders by you—and in no uncertain terms.'

'How could you have listened to me—when I loved you so much?' she raged, oblivious of what she was saying as she flung herself in anguish against him.

'Jackie, have you any idea of what you've just said?' he demanded hoarsely, his fingers biting into her flesh as he drew her from him, forcing her to look at him.

'It's obvious, isn't it?' she sobbed. 'I loved you then . . . I love you now . . . oh, God, what am I saying?'

'The words I'd almost despaired of ever hearing you say . . . Jackie, are you really saying them?' he whispered frantically, his arms fierce and possessive as they suddenly enfolded her.

'Of course I love you,' she sobbed against the face nuzzling frantically against hers, while her arms clung with all the strength of her love.

'I don't believe you're saying it,' he whispered wildly, his lips searching distractedly against her cheek. 'I've been going out of my mind since you left—since before you left. Jackie, I love you so much I find it impossible to think logically . . . you're all that fills my mind,' he protested, the desperation in his voice triggering wild explosions of happiness among the ghosts of confusion still lingering in her mind.

'Oh, Cal, you'd better start believing I love you,' she whispered tremulously, her hands gentle and comforting as they tried to dispel the desperation in him. 'I've loved you for so long, yet I was too confused to see it until that last night we made love . . .'

'I knew what you felt,' he groaned in anguish, rocking her fiercely to him. 'The love between us filled every part of me, yet even then I managed to convince myself I was imagining it . . . that I was confusing the dependency that had grown between us with love. I went on telling myself that, even though I felt as though something in me had died when you said you were free of me.' As he spoke, the pressure of his arms increased almost painfully as he sank back against the pillows, drawing her down with him.

'Cal, it doesn't matter any more,' she whispered tenderly.

'How can you say that—when I behaved so abominably?' he groaned. 'Even my own brother can hardly bring himself to speak to me.'

'You're exaggerating,' she chided lovingly, nothing but happiness inside her now, a dazzling explosion of joy that trembled on the lips that tenderly kissed his frowning brow.

'I'm not. The day you left, he suddenly got it into his head that you loved me . . . we nearly came to blows when I told him he was a fool. But I was the fool,' he whispered huskily. 'Oh, Jackie, there hasn't been a day, since you left, that hasn't been like a long, slow torture.'

'But it's over now,' she whispered, her hands gently caressing the head that lowered to lie against her breast. 'How I wish you'd listened to your very intuitive brother, though,' she added wistfully.

'My brother—and Marie; Claudia, too,' he
groaned burying his face closer against her. 'It was
Claudia who, once she had forgiven me for my unforgivable behaviour, told me to accept the fact that I
was in love . . . I told her she was mad. Then Marie
came out with pretty much the same thing a few days
later . . . I refused to discuss the cancellation of our
engagement . . . she asked me if I had ever looked—
really looked—at those engagement photographs . . .'

'I felt that anyone with eyes would be able to see
how much I loved you in those,' whispered Jackie.

'Marie felt that anyone with eyes would have been
able to see how much we both loved each other,' he
sighed. 'She told me that in no uncertain terms just
before I left for Italy . . . I got roaring drunk before I
could pick up the phone to ring you. Even then, the
words refused to come out.' He gave a soft,
disbelieving groan. 'Jackie, would you mind telling
me again that you love me? It still refuses to sink in.'

'I love you,' she murmured contentedly, happiness
a never-ending explosion within her. 'We have all
day—so you're not moving from here till I have you
convinced.'

'Not all day,' he whispered softly, rising to look
into her eyes. 'At least, I hope it's not just a day. I'm
hoping it will be the rest of our lives.' He reached out
to stroke her face, almost as though to convince himself she was real. Then he startled her by grinning, a
wicked, teasing grin that sent her heart thudding out
of control. 'Hang on a moment.' He heaved himself
away from her, then lay his cheek against her
stomach. 'Hey, you in there,' he whispered softly.
'This is your father speaking. Your mama and I

haven't too good a record when it comes to saying what's in our hearts—but your papa's about to change all that, and you're my witness.' With a gentle pat to her stomach, he hauled himself back up to her side. 'Why are you crying?' he chided softly.

'Am I crying?' she whispered, her arms encircling his neck.

'You're crying. How can I be expected to propose to a soggy . . .'

'How can you be expected to what?' she gasped, scarcely daring to breathe.

'Jackie, I love you. I want you to marry me. I want you to marry me the soonest moment possible—and not to accommodate the little miracle we've created —but because I can't bear the thought of life without you . . . Jackie, aren't you going to say anything?' he demanded impatiently.

'I was too lost in your beautiful, romantic words,' she sighed blissfully, giving a startled yelp as he suddenly disappeared from her arms and returned to consult her stomach.

'I think we have a problem here,' he confided. 'She's not answering me . . .'

'Of course I'm answering you, my crazy, wonderful idiot,' she murmured huskily, tugging him back to her. 'And the answer's positively and absolutely yes!'

'Stop beating about the bush,' he growled happily, sweeping her fiercely into his arms. 'Oh, Jackie, is it really possible to be this happy? Why didn't fireworks explode the moment you tripped so primly into my life and turned it upside-down in every conceivable way?'

'They probably did and we didn't notice them —we're quite good at that,' she murmured contentedly, her contentment turning to a shiver of excitement as his lips began nuzzling and exploring.

'We *were* quite good at that,' he corrected. 'But that's all in the past now . . . Jackie?'

'Mmm?' She shivered, distracted by the familiar sweet excitement wrought by his suddenly impatient hands.

'You won't have to wear the de Perregaux knuckle-duster, I'll get you the most beautiful ring in the world.

'How dare you refer to the most beautiful ring in the world as a knuckle-duster,' she murmured, a breathless, distracted murmur.

'But you were the one who called it that—I thought you hated it.' His chuckle caught in his throat as her hands began retaliating.

'What I hated was the thought of someone other than me ever wearing it. I loved it! Oh Cal, I love *you* so much! Cal?'

'Mmm?'

'What made you decide to come here yesterday? Why did you leave it so long?'

'Because it was the day I was leaving Los Angeles that I rang Marie yet again—she relented and gave me your ghastly solicitor's address—but only after I'd admitted that I loved you.'

'Why did you get drunk?'

'Because I was scared witless you might turn me away . . . Jackie?'

'Cal?'

'Could we cut the cross-examination, my darling? I'm a man sorely in need of convincing he's loved . . . you say you love me, but I happen know it's impossible for you to love me as much as I love you . . . as I'll always love you. No one could love anyone that much,' he murmured huskily, passion and laughter mingling in his eyes.

She took a breath, preparing to retaliate indignantly, but the breath became a soft gasp of longing as his lips and hands began studiously wreaking their exciting devastation.

And because there was nothing she wanted more, she set about proving just how wrong his words had been.

Harlequin Presents

Coming Next Month

1199 THE ALOHA BRIDE Emma Darcy
Robyn is at a low point in her life and is determined not to be hurt again. Then she meets Julian Lassiter. Somehow she finds herself wanting to solve Julian's problems in a way that is not only reckless but is positively dangerous!

1200 FANTASY LOVER Sally Heywood
Torrin Anthony's arrival in Merril's life is unwanted and upsetting, for this shallow, artificial actor reminds her of Azur—the heroic rebel sympathizer who'd rescued her from cross fire in the Middle East. Could she possibly be mixing fantasy with reality?

1201 WITHOUT TRUST Penny Jordan
Lark Cummings, on trial for crimes she's innocent of, hasn't a chance when she is faced with James Wolfe's relentless prosecution. Then the case is inexplicably dropped. She wants to hate this formidable man, but finds it impossible when fate brings him back into her life!

1202 DESPERATION Charlotte Lamb
Megan accepts a year apart from her newfound love, Devlin Hurst—she'll wait for him. Yet when her life turns upside down just hours after his departure, she knows she must break their pact. Only she has to lie to do it....

1203 TAKE AWAY THE PRIDE Emma Richmond
Toby lies about her qualifications to become secretary to powerful Marcus du Mann—and is a disaster. But when Marcus gets stuck with his baby nephew, Toby is put in charge. And she's coping well—until Marcus decides to move in and help....

1204 TOKYO TRYST Kay Thorpe
Two years ago, Alex walked out on Greg Wilde when she discovered he was unfaithful. Now they're on the same work assignment in Japan. Despite Greg's obvious interest in the beautiful Yuki, Alex finds herself falling in love with him all over again!

1205 IMPULSIVE GAMBLE Lynn Turner
Free-lance journalist Abbie desperately wants a story on reclusive engineer-inventor Malacchi Garrett. Then she discovers the only way to get close to him is by living a lie. But how can she lie to the man she's falling in love with?

1206 NO GENTLE LOVING Sara Wood
Hostile suspicion from wealthy Dimitri Kastelli meets Helen in Crete, where she's come to find out about the mother she never knew. What grudge could he hold against a long-dead peasant woman? And how would he react if he learned who Helen is?

Available in September wherever paperback books are sold, or through Harlequin Reader Service:

In the U.S.
901 Fuhrmann Blvd.
P.O. Box 1397
Buffalo, N.Y. 14240-1397

In Canada
P.O. Box 603
Fort Erie, Ontario
L2A 5X3

Harlequin American Romance®

The sun, the surf, the sand...

One relaxing month by the sea was all Zoe, Diana and Gracie ever expected from their four-week stay at Gull Cottage, the luxurious East Hampton mansion. They never thought that what they found at the beach would change their lives forever.

Join Zoe, Diana and Gracie for the summer of their lives. Don't miss the GULL COTTAGE trilogy in Harlequin American Romance: #301 CHARMED CIRCLE by Robin Francis (July 1989); #305 MOTHER KNOWS BEST by Barbara Bretton (August 1989); and #309 SAVING GRACE by Anne McAllister (September 1989).

GULL COTTAGE—because one month can be the start of forever...

GULLG-1